Praise for the Casson Family stories:

'Hilary McKay is always funny, touching and surprising, and depths of wisdom despite her lightness of touch. She makes us ca about these characters as we would about what happens to members of our own family.' Nicolette Jones, *The Sunday Times*

'. . touching and hilarious. Beautifully crafted descriptive language this offering a real gem.' *School Library Journal*

'Sa. s Angel is a delight from start to finish . . . a great feel-good boo with characters you want to stay with for ever. Warm, beautifully crafted and always original, it's pure fun – a book to recommend without hesitation.' Whitbread Judges, as reported in e *Daily Mail*

'McKay's strength lies in her understanding of young people and her ability to evoke them very simply.' *The Guardian*

'. . a welcome new instalment in the lives of the unforgettable Casson family . . . the characters of every Casson child go on developing.' *The Independent* magazine

'Permanent Rose is the antidote to everything that's bad in children's books and, indeed, everything that's bad in life.' *The Sunday Telegraph*

'. . McKay treats us once again to one of her brilliantly characterised families. This is a really lovely book.' *The Bookseller*

'McKay has many strengths . . . McKay has clarity of style and a sophistication of approach that almost make the book as right for a nearly nine-year-old like Rose as for a 15-year-old like Saffy. And it's a joy for an adult to read, too.' *Books for Keeps*

'Hilary McKay excels in conveying the anarchic bedlam of family life, and she has excelled herself in her marvellous novel, Saffy's Angel which deserves to be placed alongside such classics as Little Women and The Railway Children.' *TES Primary*

Hilary McKay

Caddy
Ever After

Hodder Children's Books

A division of Hachette Children's Books

First published in Great Britain in 2006
by Hodder Children's Books

This paperback edition published in 2007

The poem 'The Tree of Life' from the anthology *Love of Ireland –
Poems from the Irish* by Brendan Kennelly has been reprinted
by kind permission of Mercier Press Ltd., Cork.

1

A Catalogue record for this book is available from
the British Library

ISBN-10: 0 340 90315 5

Typeset in Bembo by Avon DataSet Ltd,
Bidford on Avon, Warwickshire

Printed and bound in Great Britain by
Clays Ltd, St Ives plc

The paper and board used in this paperback by Hodder Children's
Books are natural recyclable products made from wood grown in
sustainable forests. The manufacturing processes conform to the
environmental regulations of the country of origin.

Hodder Children's Books
a division of Hachette Children's Books
338 Euston Road
London NW1 3BH

For Kirsten and Vivian

THE FLYING FEELING

by

Rose Casson

Class 4

The Flying Feeling

Today I fell asleep in class. School had hardly begun (it was Literacy Hour). Miss Farley, my class teacher, touched me on my shoulder to wake me up.

'NO, NO,' I shouted very loudly, and fell on the floor and crawled under the table to escape.

Then I realised where I was, so I came out and sat down again as quietly as I could. I hoped that if I was quick and quiet enough Miss Farley almost would not notice I had done anything unusual. But she did.

Miss Farley said, 'Rose, is there anything wrong? Here at school? Or at home, perhaps?'

I could tell by the way she looked at me that she had not forgotten about yesterday.

Why I Fell Asleep In Class
A Long Thought
By Rose Casson
Class 4
(Part 1)

Miss Farley has a big cheek asking me if there is anything wrong like that. In front of everyone. How would she like it if I did it to her? On one of those days when she comes in with little eyes and no lipstick and snaps, 'Right Class 4, we will separate these groups of tables into lines, since you cannot seem to behave as you are! Rose Casson, what is so interesting out of that window?' (Sky.) 'Also, Rose, since when have tie-dyed T-shirts been school uniform, may I ask? And before you do anything, go to the office and take out that earring and ask them for a recycled envelope to put it in, please.'

On those days, do I ask, 'Miss Farley, is there anything wrong at home? Or at school, perhaps?'

No.

Luckily, she has not noticed my earring today. It is a gold hoop with dangling red crystals on gold links. My sister Saffron gave it to me this morning.

There is a clean patch on the carpet in the Reading Corner where one of the carpet tiles has been shampooed. So nobody in the class can forget about yesterday either.

Also Ghost Club has been banned.

Ghost Club

On wet lunch breaks at our school you can either go to the hall and play, or stay in your classroom and be as quiet as mice. (If mice are like hamsters, they are not very quiet.) That is when we do Ghost Club – Kiran (who used to be my best friend) and me and some of the others.

For Ghost Club we turn off the lights and pull down the blinds as far as they will go and sit in a circle on the floor, on the carpet tiles in the Reading Corner. Then we very, very quietly, very quietly, really quietly take turns to tell ghost stories.

Yesterday was a rainy day, and so we did Ghost Club. First Molly told us about her grandad whose false teeth slid out when he fell asleep watching football.

'I don't think that sounds very scary,' I said.

'Yes, well, OK, it is only slightly scary,' agreed Molly, 'but admit it is totally gross!'

I admitted this at once, and then I told about the strange scratchy noises in our house at night which cannot be my sister Caddy's escaped hamsters because they would have died ages ago. According to the Hamster Book.

Everyone at Ghost Club said their houses made strange noises at night too, which their mothers told them were caused by Central Heating. I explained that we did not have Central Heating.

Kiran hummed like she was bored and picked at a carpet tile and said, 'All houses creak a bit and you can get false-tooth glue to keep them in, they advertise it on daytime TV when they know old people are watching. You know my cousin? No, carry on talking about Central Heating! Maybe I shouldn't tell you!'

So of course we made her tell us.

Kiran's stories are the worst because they are true. They are all about people in her family.

I used to think, Thank goodness I am not related to Kiran. If I was related to Kiran I would not feel safe.

Terrible things happen all the time to that family.

'Which cousin?' we asked Kiran, because her family (as well as being unsafe) is enormous.

'My cousin who doesn't go to this school with the pink jacket,' Kiran told us. 'You know that one?'

'No,' we said.

'Well, you know my auntie who came on visitors' day who had to have all the windows opened very quickly?'

'Yes,' we said.

'That's her mother. She bought my cousin the pink jacket. From the market stall next to the mobile ear-piercing van. And anyway, you know that place by the park near Rose's house where no one is allowed to go?'

'No,' we said.

'Yes you do, it is all fenced in and a notice says: DANGER HIGH VOLTAGE.'

'It is an electricity substation,' said Molly, who always knows stuff like that because she goes on Intelligent Quality Time Walks with her mother. (I don't.)

'Well,' continued Kiran very quickly, before Molly could start telling us about substations, 'my cousin with the pink jacket was walking past that place and it was winter and it was nearly dark and you know how if you hold your hand up very close to your face and it is nearly dark, all the fingers look thick and black and not real?'

We said no, and then we tried it with our own hands sitting in the nearly-darkness of the Reading Corner, and then we said, 'Oh yes.'

'A hand like that but much bigger,' said Kiran. She is speaking very quietly indeed now, like she does not

8

really want us to hear. 'Over her shoulder. And no footprints. No sound of footprints. And not quite touching her. My cousin. And the fingers very thick and dark like a thick dark leather glove. Not smooth leather. Reaching over her shoulder, just at that place by the park where you are not allowed to go. She saw it out of the corner of her eye.'

Nobody said anything.

'She just caught sight of it for a moment. The first time.'

You could hear the clock and the sound of people being told off in the hall and you could hear us breathing.

'But she saw it for longer the next time.'

'Did she look around?' whispered Molly.

'Only once.'

'What did she see?'

'She won't tell me.'

'Ki … raaan!' we wailed.

'So now she won't wear her pink jacket and my auntie says it is a waste because it was nearly new and she says I can have it and wear it with a scarf. Because they won't wash off; they are burnt on.'

'*WHAT* ARE BURNT ON?' shouted several people.

'The fingermarks,' said Kiran, sounding very

surprised that we did not know. 'The thick burnt-brown fingermarks on the shoulder of the jacket.'

We didn't say anything.

'I'm not having that revolting jacket,' said Kiran.

Still nobody said anything. We were thinking. We knew the place by the park where you are not allowed to go. We knew Kiran's auntie who bought the jacket, and we knew the market stall it came from. We even knew the mobile ear-piercing van; my sister Saffron had her nose pierced there. When I thought about it, I thought I even knew Kiran's cousin who doesn't go to this school. And I knew, exactly as if I had seen them, what the thick dark fingermarks looked like scorched on to the shoulder of that pink jacket.

Someone grabbed my shoulder very hard and shouted, 'ROSE'S TURN!'

I jumped so badly I felt sick and dizzy, and I shouted, 'Not me!' without even meaning to shout, but I don't think it sounded very loud. Everyone was laughing so much.

Kiran said, 'I am sorry Rose, I am sorry Rose, I am sorry Rose!' but I will never forgive her.

If I had a choice between dying and wetting myself in class, I would choose dying.

Hamsters

These are the people who live at my house:

1. Me.

2. Mummy, who is called Eve. She is an artist. She does her art in a shed at the bottom of the garden. It is not true that Mummy calls everyone darling to save her bothering to remember names.

3. Indigo, who is my brother and is five years older than me. Indigo is very tall and thin. With his eyes closed he looks dead. He always has, but no one has ever got used to it. This is bad luck for Indigo. It means that ever since he was a baby, frightened people have been shaking him awake to make sure he is still alive. Over the years Indigo has grown more and more difficult to wake up.

4. Saffron. She is really my cousin, but she is my adopted sister too. She is nearly fifteen and she is very pretty (like Caddy) and very clever (like Indigo). When Saffron

found out about yesterday at Ghost Club she said, 'One way of getting the carpet cleaned, Rosy Pose!'

Saffron is ruthless.

These are the people who do not live at my house:
1. Daddy. He lives in London where he has a studio. Because he is an artist too. (He says.)
2. My grown-up sister Caddy who is at university. Before she went to university she kept more guinea pigs and hamsters than most people would want to own. She kept them all over the place. There are still some guinea pigs left in a hutch in the garden, but the hamsters are all gone.

But where have they gone?

Yesterday evening when my sister Saffron was doing her homework and my brother Indigo was lying on the floor listening to terrible music with his headphones on (this is still about why I fell asleep in class), I told Mummy what happened at school. She was making an illuminated manuscript because she is having a display of illuminated manuscripts in the library. Poems in old-fashioned writing with little pictures around the capital letters and decorated edges. On this poem she was drawing singing birds, all different bright colours among the leaves.

'I know darling Bill would say it is Not Exactly Art,' she said. (Darling Bill is Daddy.) 'But it is fun and they sell amazingly well and the suspension on my car has more or less gone completely. These days it is more like sledging along on your bottom than real driving, so I will have to get it fixed and goodness knows what it will cost. Do you like the poem, Rosy Pose? It is tenth century Irish. Translated. Caddy used to have accidents at school so often that I put dry knickers in every morning with her packed lunch. Until she started school dinners.'

Then there was a big bang and all the lights went out.

'Goodness,' said Mummy, after a minute or two. 'Or is it just one bulb?'

Indigo continued to lie on the floor with his eyes shut, droning away to his terrible music, because he was running on batteries.

'No it isn't just one bulb,' said Mummy, futilely flicking switches. 'It is all over the house.'

Then she accidentally trod on Indigo and he unplugged himself and said, 'Candles.'

'I know,' said Mummy. 'But unfortunately not. I threw them all away after I had a terrible dream about Rose accidentally setting the house on fire.

In case it was a warning. And I took that big
cinnamon-scented one into college to relax my Young
Offenders only last week –' Mummy teaches Art to
Young Offenders – so that they can do their
vandalising with style and confidence, Daddy says '–
and it is still there.'

'Did it relax them?' enquired Indigo.

'Yes and no,' said Mummy. 'I had to blow it out
because a very naughty little boy used it to light up
a . . . Well, never mind! He was surprised that I
recognised the smell. (Poor darling.) I wonder if the
power is off in the shed?'

Indigo said he would go and see and he went outside
and did, and it wasn't because the shed was properly
wired by an intelligent hippy who lived in a tent and
who (briefly) fell in love with Caddy and then
Mummy. He unblocked the sink too. But soon after
that he went to Tangier in an old bus. His name was
Derek, and he would have taken Mummy to Tangier
with him, and me and Indy and Saffron too, and Caddy
could have visited for holidays. There was plenty of
room in the bus. But we didn't go. Because Mummy
said, 'What about darling Bill?'

And Derek said there wasn't that much room in
the bus.

What has this got to do with why I fell asleep in class?

Everything.

But what has it got to do with hamsters?

We didn't find out till morning.

Mummy said, 'Oh good, that solves everything!' when she heard there was still power in the shed.

Mummy would be perfectly happy to live in the shed.

Saffron, Sarah, Orlando Bloom and the Dark

Indigo found two torches, one for him and one for me, and he gave me the brightest because you do not need much light to listen to music. It is best in the dark.

Mummy went out to do her illuminated manuscript in the shed, and Saffron came groping and grumbling down the stairs because of her homework.

'This is so not a good time to be plunged into darkness,' she said, flapping her hands about. 'Where has everyone gone?'

'I am here,' I said, shining my torch in my face so she screamed. 'And Mummy is in the shed where it is still light and Indy is on the floor beside me. It is a power cut.'

'If there is still light in the shed then it is not a power cut,' said Saffron. 'It is an Electrical Problem in this house. Right in the middle of my maths homework

16

and I have just varnished my nails and they are still sticky.' (That was why she was flapping her hands so much. To dry her nails.) 'It is not fair. I wanted to get 100% because we have a new student teacher for maths until the end of term and he looks exactly like Orlando Bloom only without the bow and arrows and gold teeth and sandals, and he will be marking it.'

She said this while groping her way very carefully to the phone so as not to ruin her nails. 'I am ringing up Sarah,' said Saffron. (Sarah is her best friend.) 'I bet they haven't got a power cut.'

So she did and they hadn't.

Then Saffron and Sarah had a huge conversation in the dark (at our end) about nail varnish and maths homework and gold teeth, and it ended up an argument.

'Why do best friends argue so much more than ordinary friends?' I asked Indigo, whose batteries were going flat.

'Because they listen to each other so much more than ordinary friends,' said Indigo.

Sarah's house is very close to ours, just down the road, past the park. After the telephone argument Saffron went to Sarah's house to prove she was right. She took her maths homework with her, and her nail varnish, and her night things, because Sarah's mother

said she and Sarah's father were going out and would
not be back till late and if Saffron would like to stay the
night, that would be perfect.

I like Sarah's mother. She always makes you feel like
just the person she was hoping to see. Especially if you
go round at meal times, when she says, 'Wonderful!
I have cooked far too much for just us,' and gets
out extra bread and salad and lets me hunt in the
freezer for pudding.

It is easy to stay the night at Sarah's house because
Sarah has an enormous bedroom with two beds and a
hammock in it. Ever since I first saw it I have wanted
to sleep in Sarah's hammock.

When Saffron had gone, the house felt very lonely
indeed. And dark. Especially when Indigo took the
batteries out of his torch and put them in his CD
player. Then we only had one working torch left.

'What can you do when it is as dark as this?'
I asked Indigo.

'Go to bed,' said Indigo.

After a while I did go to bed. Mummy wasn't
coming back into the house, I knew. She would finish
her manuscript and then she would lie down on the
old pink sofa she keeps in her shed, and then she
would accidentally fall asleep, and she would still be
there in the morning.

I hate it when Mummy goes to sleep in the shed by accident.

Especially when there is no one in the house except Indigo and me.

And the lights don't work.

And it has been a horrible day.

The Lightning in the Shed
(Part 1)

When I was in bed I tried very hard not to think about what happened to me in the Reading Corner, and about Kiran's cousin's pink jacket, and the dark unreal hand over her shoulder, and the way she looked back once and would not tell Kiran what she saw. And how Kiran's quiet voice sounded when she said, 'I don't want that revolting jacket.'

It was very hard not to think of these things. So I concentrated on what I could hear – and there were sounds in the walls. Scrabbly sounds, like giant spiders would make. I got up and made Indigo turn his music off and come and listen.

'Nope,' said Indigo. 'I can't hear a thing. Not a single spider. Not a leg. Go back to bed, Rosy Pose.'

I went back to bed, and to stop myself listening I felt my neck to see if I had any lumps growing there.

Kiran's cousin once had a lump on her neck. Not the cousin with the jacket, another cousin with very long hair. She got the lump when she went on holiday to a very hot place where she bought Kiran a bracelet made of shells and silver beads and string which Kiran used to wear to school until the string got dirty. And then she washed it and all the silver came off the beads and they were plastic underneath.

At first Kiran's cousin's lump was little, but it got bigger. It grew. I know exactly where. On the back of her neck, just where her head joins on. I have a little mole in the same place. And the lump grew and it itched, but Kiran's cousin's hair covered it up and she did not tell anyone, and it grew bigger. And then one day when Kiran's cousin was brushing her hair she banged the lump with her hairbrush and it opened. And Kiran's cousin screamed and screamed and out poured spiders. Dozens and dozens of black spiders.

I got out of bed again and went to Indigo's room and asked Indigo to check my neck for spider lumps.

He checked very carefully and patiently and he said there were none at all, and he said the sounds I could hear were probably hamsters in the walls.

'Maybe it is Joseph,' said Indigo. Joseph was a hamster

with fur which was all different colours (which was why he was called Joseph). 'Or Blossom,' said Indigo. (Blossom had a white flower-shaped mark in the middle of her back.)

But Joseph and Blossom escaped long ago, and hamsters do not live very long. They would have died by now. We have a Hamster Book which explains this. And if they had not died they would have killed each other because that is what hamsters do. They fight to the death. The Hamster Book says that too. So.

I told Indigo this and he said, 'But Joseph and Blossom have not read the Hamster Book. So you never know. Go back to bed, Rosy Pose.'

I went back to bed, and I thought about Joseph and Blossom.

Somewhere, Joseph and Blossom are dead in this house.

This was not a nice thought, and as soon as I had thought it I wished I hadn't. I especially wished I had not thought the word HOUSE.

It reminded me of what happened to another of Kiran's aunties.

She used to have a dream. It was a dream of a house that she had never seen. A lovely house, in the country. She dreamed of it so often, and for so many years, that it felt like her own house, even though she had never been there in real life.

And then one day when she was driving in the country she saw it. Her house. Exactly like her dreams. And it was for sale.

So Kiran's aunt stopped her car and she jumped out and she ran to the gate, and across the sunny garden and up to the house, just as she had run so many times in her dreams. And she knocked at the door.

A man opened it and he stared at Kiran's aunt.

'Oh please,' she said, 'please tell me. Is this house really for sale?'

'Yes,' he said, staring and staring, and shaking too. Shaking and grey. 'Yes, it is. But you wouldn't want to buy it.'

'Why not?' asked Kiran's aunt.

'It's haunted,' said the man.

'Haunted?' said Kiran's aunt, and she laughed.

'Don't laugh,' said the man.

But Kiran's aunt still laughed and she said, 'Is it haunted often?'

'Yes,' said the man. 'Often. Often. As it has been for years. You should know. YOU ARE THE GHOST THAT HAUNTS THIS HOUSE!'

Then the man fell down dead on the doorstep.

Then Kiran's poor aunt ran screaming away across

the sunny garden and out into the road and straight under a lorry that was coming from the quarry round the corner.

And it killed her.

Indigo was very grumpy when I woke him up to tell him this story, and he said, 'If the man at the door died and Kiran's aunt died, then how does Kiran know anything about it?'

'Of course she knows about it,' I said. 'It was her aunt. Indigo, do you think this house is haunted?'

'No,' said Indigo. 'This is the least haunted house in the world. There's always someone awake in it. Or being shaken awake. You are quite safe. And Saffy is safe at Sarah's. And Mum is safe in the shed. So go back to bed, Rosy Pose.'

The Lightning in the Shed (Part 2)

But *is* Mummy safe in the shed?

There is no lock on the door of the shed.

Indigo has never been so hard to wake up but I managed it in the end, and at last he sat up all sleepy and groaning and he said, 'Now what?'

I said, 'What if someone comes in the night and murders Mummy in the shed?'

Indigo was not cross but he was not very interested either. He said, 'What would be the point?'

'Murderers do not need a point,' I said. 'They do it for fun.'

'I don't think it would be much fun murdering Mum in the shed,' said Indigo.

'But you are not a murderer,' I pointed out.

Indigo made a growling noise and pulled his quilt

over his head, but then he pulled it off again and said, 'I do not think Mum is in any danger of being murdered in the shed. I think she has less chance of being murdered in the shed than she has of being struck by lightning.'

This cheered me up at once because although I have always been slightly worried about Mum being murdered in the shed, I have never been the slightest bit afraid of her being struck by lightning.

'If you are really scared,' said Indigo (who had got his eyes open now), 'I will take you to the shed to check she has not been murdered. Or struck by lightning. But,' (he pulled back the curtain beside his bed and looked out) 'it is raining.'

'Is it thundering?' I asked.

'No,' said Indigo. 'It is just plain raining. It is not thundering or lightning.'

'Then we will leave her where she is,' I said.

'Oh good,' said Indigo.

Then put his headphones on.

Next he put his head under his pillow.

After that, he pulled his quilt over his pillow.

From underneath he said, 'Don't wake me up again please, Rosy Pose.'

The Lightning in the Shed
(Part 3)

I went back to bed and thought about things.

Nothing good.

And I must have fallen asleep.

I know I must have fallen asleep, because I remember dreaming. I dreamed that lorries were driving over the roof of the house, dragging huge chains behind them like snail trails. I could still hear them when I woke up. It sounded like thunder.

It *was* thunder. And the rain was much harder now than it had been before. It was hitting my bedroom window with a rattle like stones, but I think it was the lightning that woke me up. The lightning was so bright I could see the flashes with my eyes shut.

And the power was off.

And Saffy was at Sarah's house.

And Indigo would not wake up.

And Mummy was asleep in the shed.

Afterwards, Saffy gave me this earring that Miss Farley has not noticed yet, as a reward for my bravery in going to rescue Mummy from the lightning in the shed.

Sometimes when people get rewards for bravery they say, 'Oh I was not really brave. I do not deserve a reward. Anyone would have done the same.'

But it was not like that for me. I was very brave. I think I did deserve a reward. Because it was very scary going downstairs in the dark to rescue Mummy, and as I crossed the living-room floor my bare toe touched something warm and limp and furry, and I saw by a flash of lightning that it was Joseph's ghost.

I rushed across the room to the kitchen, and then I crossed the kitchen and opened the back door. When I saw exactly what it was like outside I nearly didn't go any further.

But I did.

When I went outside I was wearing:
1. My pyjamas.
2. Indigo's denim jacket.
3. Saffy's old trainers.

I found the jacket and the trainers in the kitchen by lightning because the power was still off.

There was no light on in the shed. I would have to wake Mummy up before I could rescue her.

Outside, the rain was so cold it hurt and the wind had gone mad and was blowing in four directions at once, tearing at Indigo's jacket as if it knew he had not said I could wear it. But worst of all were Saffy's trainers. They were much too big so that although I wanted more than anything to run, I had to walk quite slowly. Behind me the kitchen door banged shut. I wrapped my arms tight around myself and shuffled along the garden path.

Mummy was not in the shed.

The shed was just the same, with the canvases toppling against the walls, and jam jars full of paintbrushes, and the little yellow table with the kettle and the jar of instant coffee and the bag of guinea pig food. The pink sofa was there, with the old quilt Mummy brought back from India, but Mummy was not asleep on it.

I thought of murderers at once and I shut my eyes very tightly in case there was blood.

Then I opened them, and there was no blood.

There is nowhere in the shed that anyone could hide

except under the sofa, but there was no one under the sofa. I know because I checked.

Anyone who checks under a sofa in a shed in a thunderstorm in the middle of the night for either:

1. Their mother's body

or

2. Whoever got their mother

is very brave indeed.

That was me.

After I had checked under the sofa I started looking round the shed for clues. It seemed to me that if Mummy was not in the shed, then someone or something must have got her. I could not rescue her if I did not know who, or what. That was why I looked for clues.

The only thing different or new was the illuminated poem on the table. It was finished now, the colours red and green and blue and gold all very bright and clear. Mummy says when she does her decorated poems, 'The trick is not to make them look like wallpaper.'

This one did not look like wallpaper, but I did not look at it properly because I was having another horrible thought. I was thinking whoever (or whatever) got Mummy might now come back for me.

In nearly no time at all, I kicked off Saffy's trainers and got out of that shed and back to the house.

(This is still about why I fell asleep in class.)

I got back to the house, and that was the worst problem yet.

The door was shut. I had heard it shut as I went to the shed, but I was concentrating so much on rescuing Mummy from the lightning and not falling over in Saffron's trainers that I had not really noticed. The door has the sort of lock that locks itself when it shuts, and this had happened and I was locked out.

Now the lightning was flashing so often that it was on more than it was off, and the thunder and the rain were stronger than ever, and I was locked out, and I rang the doorbell and rang the doorbell and rang the doorbell and Indigo did not come.

And then I remembered that it was an electric doorbell and so of course it was not working.

How wrong I was to think that I was safe because all the terrible things happened to Kiran's family.

The Lightning in the Shed
(Part 4)

I had not stopped being brave yet (although I would have liked to). I had to decide what to do, and these were my choices:

1. Go back to the shed and wait for whatever got Mummy to come and get me.

2. Sit on the doorstep and wait for whatever got Mummy to come and get me OR to be struck by lightning.

3. Run for help to Sarah's house.

The trouble with running for help to Sarah's house was that on the way I risked being got by whatever got Mummy AND being struck by lightning AND, as well, the way to Sarah's house is past the park and the place where it says DANGER HIGH VOLTAGE and you are not allowed to go. And I had not forgotten that this was the place where the hand reached out. The hand that scorched the pink jacket of Kiran's cousin who does not go to our school.

But I could not bear to go back to the shed, and it was terrible on the doorstep, and I thought I might survive the journey to Sarah's house because I can run very fast (only not in Saffron's trainers).

It takes about three minutes to walk to Sarah's house, but if you run in bare feet in a thunderstorm in the middle of the night with you-don't-know-what behind you and even worse in front it takes about a minute and a half. This is what I did, and I was past the place where it said DANGER HIGH VOLTAGE before I had hardly taken a breath.

And then I could not help it. I looked back.

There is a cherry tree just behind the DANGER HIGH VOLTAGE place, and its branches hang low over the pavement and one has been trimmed so that it looks just like a hand. A dark hand with bent fingers in thick leather gloves.

But it was only a branch of cherry tree.

Of course I shall not tell that to the Horror Club (which I intend to start as soon as possible).

I shall say, 'How lucky it is that I was wearing Indigo's jacket, which is blacky-brown and does not show scorch marks.'

And I shall not tell them that as soon as I knew

Kiran's cousin's terrible hand was a branch of cherry tree, I knew something else too.

I knew where Mummy was.

In bed.

Humans cannot fly, but they can get the flying feeling. All they need to do is go out at night into a wild storm where the thunder roars like applause and the lightning throws itself in daggers of light at your bare feet, and you suddenly find you are not afraid.

Saffron and Sarah were not asleep. They were watching the storm from Sarah's bedroom window and they saw me at once, so that before I could reach the front door of the house it was open, and Saffron and Sarah, and Sarah's parents too, were all pulling me inside.

And I was quite right, Mummy was in bed. Sarah's mother rang up and found out.

Then everyone had hot chocolate except Sarah's father (who had whisky), and I had a hot bath too. And afterwards Saffron and Sarah put me to bed in the hammock. You have to be put to bed in a hammock. It is impossible to do it yourself, but it is lovely when you are in.

Sarah's mother turned the light off and she said, 'You are my favourite guest, Rose, but it is after three o'clock in the morning. I will make you pancakes for breakfast if you go to sleep this second WITH NO MORE FUSS.'

So I did.

Why I Fell Asleep In Class
A Long Thought
By Rose Casson
Class 4
(Part 2)

'Tired people cannot learn,' said Miss Farley, dumping a handful of marker pens into a full mug of coffee and trying to look like she had meant to do it.

But that is not true. Tired people *can* learn (and learning is tiring). I am very tired and I have learned a lot since yesterday.

Things I Have Learned Since Yesterday

1. Hamsters
Hamsters do not always do what it says in the Hamster

Book. Because after Joseph and Blossom escaped, they made friends and lived wild in the house and had a lot of children. And they lived for twice as long as they were meant to do, and Joseph chewed through the television cable and caused a power cut which temporarily stunned him until I touched him with my foot and woke him up. It was not his ghost after all, it was the real Joseph. Indigo found him in the living room this morning, asleep under a sofa cushion. As soon as Joseph saw Indigo he ran off. Indigo said he looked slightly guilty but otherwise perfectly well.

2. Kiran's family

Maybe it is true that Kiran's family have all the terrible things happen to them. But maybe not. Because at breakfast time, while we were eating pancakes, I told everyone the things Kiran had told us at Ghost Club. And Sarah's mother said, 'Oh, the spider story! I had forgotten the spider story!'

'Do you know Kiran's cousin?' I asked, very surprised.

'No,' said Sarah's mother, 'but I know that story! I heard it when I was a little girl with long hair. I was told it by my brother who had a friend who had a sister who still had the scar to prove it!'

She knew the one about Kiran's aunty and the

dream house too. 'Those stories have been old for a very long time,' she said. 'I am glad to hear they are still being told. Your friend sounds an excellent storyteller!'

So maybe Kiran's family do not have all the bad luck in the world. Maybe they just have Kiran.

3. The Flying Feeling

The worst thing about coming to school this morning was the clean patch on the carpet tiles in the Reading Corner. I did not know how I could bear to look at the Reading Corner ever again. I knew that everyone else was looking at it. And remembering what happened. And I knew they always would. I know Class 4. They never forget anything.

I thought, If I don't look everyone will know why I am not looking. And I thought, If I do look everyone will know that I am trying to pretend I don't care.

All the same, I could not help looking to see how much the clean patch showed.

It showed a lot.

Everyone looked at me looking at it and they saw that I saw that it showed a lot.

Suddenly I thought of Saffron and, without realising it, I said out loud what Saffron said the night before. I said, 'I suppose it was one way of getting the carpet cleaned.'

If you can make people laugh, if you can make them *really* laugh, then they cannot laugh at you.

Also you get the Flying Feeling.

Appendices

Appendices are the extra bits at the end of a story which people might want to know. Or not. It depends whether the story is any good.

Appendix I
Why I Only Wear
One Earring

The reason I only wear one earring is that when Saffron and Sarah took me to get my ears pierced, I did not know what it would be like. They said it would not hurt much, and they were telling the truth. It did not hurt much.

'You will hear a sort of pop,' they said, 'and then it will be done.'

That was true too, I did hear a sort of pop, and then it was done, and I had a right ear that could wear earrings. But I did not like that pop. It felt like being slightly, but definitely, shot.

Nothing Saffron and Sarah could say could make me let them shoot me twice.

That is why I only wear one earring.

One is enough.

Appendix II
Mummy's Poem

I cannot tell anyone what this poem means. I do not know. I cannot explain why I like it either. But I do.

Round the tree of Life the flowers
Are ranged, abundant, even;
Its crest on every side spread out
On the fields and plains of Heaven

Glorious flocks of singing birds
Celebrate their truth,
Green abounding branches bear
Choicest leaves and fruit.

The lovely flocks maintain their song
In the changeless weather
A hundred feathers for every bird
A hundred songs for every feather.

Appendix III
Miss Farley

Miss Farley laughed as much as everyone else when I said, 'One way of getting the carpet cleaned.' Also, she stopped trying to pretend she had meant to put her pens in her cold coffee. She said, 'Good grief, look what I have done! I must be totally losing it at last. Rose, do you think you could go and get me a handful of paper towels, and while you are out pop into the office and ask for a recycled envelope to put that … Oh never mind. I will try and only see your left ear, just for today.'

At break time we noticed she put her lipstick on.

Also at break time I told Kiran about the Lightning in the Shed. Kiran said I was ten million times braver than anyone she ever knew, including her big brother's friend's big brother.

'Never heard of him,' I said.

'Yes you have,' said Kiran. 'He is the one who missed firework night because he ran three times the wrong way round a church at Halloween in order to find out what would happen.'

'What did happen?' I asked.

'Oh well,' said Kiran. 'A black thing came out of one of the graves and said, "I've been waiting a long time for a fool to come and take my place." And it rushed towards him, and he fell over and cracked his head on a tombstone and missed firework night . . .'

I have decided that Kiran just cannot help it.

It is nice being best friends again, and now there is nothing wrong anywhere, at home or at school.

THIS IS HOW
I DO SPECIAL

by

Indigo Casson

This Is How I Do Special
(Part 1)

I can only think of two things that Rose is good at. One is art and the other is loving. She is rubbish at everything else. But there is something about Rose. Of all the people I know, Rose is the only that I can imagine being famous one day.

Actually, I have just remembered another thing Rose is good at. Crime.

I hope she does not get famous for crime. I mentioned this to Saffy and Sarah, and Sarah said, 'Keep hoping! What else could she be famous for?'

It was about a week before Valentine's Day, and Rose was mass-producing Valentine's Day cards at the kitchen table. Saffron and Sarah were watching. In a disgruntled kind of way.

'Valentine's cards are supposed to be special,' said Saffron. 'You can hardly call them special if you send them off in dozens.'

'This is how I do special,' said Rose.

Here is how Rose was running her mass production.

On the table (among the uncleared Saturday-morning coffee cups and toast crumbs) she had a stack of blank folded cards, a paintbrush and some tubs of poster paint: red and white and yellow. She painted her left hand with a mixture of these colours and then she slapped it down on one of the folded cards. There was paint on the table and on Rose's face and hair and clothes. Saffron and Sarah were continually dodging splatters. They were both of them seriously grumpy.

It was not like Sarah to be like this, especially not with Rose. Sarah usually defends Rose. She usually admires her painting too, which not everyone does.

Not this time. When a peach-coloured blob of paint splattered on to her cheek, she wiped it away quite crossly and remarked Valentine's cards were for kids and grannies and if one came her way it would be put in the bin, unopened.

'Nobody need patronise me!' she said.

'What about if you were sent more than one?' asked Rose. 'What about if you were sent ten? Would you open ten?'

'No, I wouldn't,' said Sarah.

'Twenty?' asked Rose. 'You would have to open twenty!'

'Nobody gets twenty!' snapped Sarah.

'Last year,' said Rose smugly, 'I got nineteen!'

'You got nineteen,' said Saffron. 'Because your class made Valentine's Day cards for art and all the boys sent the ones they made to you! Some of them sent two. *That's* the only reason you got nineteen.'

'It was still nineteen though,' said Rose. 'So.'

She had finished her painting, and now she picked up one of the first cards she had made. Over the handprint (now dry) she drew with a thick gold felt pen one of the curly, funny, cartoon roses that she has drawn for years and years. It looked very good. The colours of the handprint made the colours of the petals of the rose.

'Who are you going to send them to?' I asked her.

'Michael,' answered Rose, adding a thorny golden stem to a yellow rose. 'The man at the music shop. Derek in Tangier. All the boys in my class. Tom.'

'And are you expecting them all to send cards back to you?' asked Saffron.

'As long as I get one from Tom,' said Rose, licking a smear of paint off her gold pen. 'Could you email him, Indy? And remind him?'

Saffron and Sarah simultaneously snorted.

'Haven't you *any* pride?' demanded Sarah.

'Me?'

'Yes.'

'About Tom?'

'Yes.'

'No,' said Rose.

Sarah suddenly stopped being nasty and hugged Rose, who was not expecting it.

'I thought you were mad with me,' she said in surprise.

'Oh, Rosy Pose!' said Sarah, laughing a bit. 'I was fed up about something, that's all. Nothing to do with you.'

'So do you really think you *would* have to open twenty Valentine's cards?'

'Don't you ever give up?' demanded Saffron.

But Sarah said, 'Yes, maybe. Yes, you are probably right. You *couldn't* not open twenty.'

After this, she and Saffron went up to the bathroom to see if there was anything in the cupboard that would remove gold ink and poster paint; Rose had been in no state to be hugged and she had come off in multicoloured patches all over Sarah's top.

I stayed, watching Rose bash out her cards. She made it look easy, but really she was doing it very carefully, drawing on her roses, and adding the stems and thorns.

'I didn't think you would bother to send cards to anyone except Tom,' I said.

Rose did not say anything for a bit, and then she said something that I did not understand at all.

'They are all for Tom really,' she said.

Sarah

Rose has found out why Sarah was so grumpy. It is because of the Valentine's Day disco at school next week.

Oh.

'But why would that make Sarah fed up?' I asked.

'Becaaaaaauuuuuse,' said Rose, like I was very thick, 'she has a wheelchair.'

So she does.

It is strange to think that there was a time when Sarah passed our house and did not wave. A time when we overtook her wheelchair as we hurried home from school, and did not speak. She knew our names a long time before we knew hers.

What is it like for a girl in a wheelchair watching other children rush by? Not strangers: familiar people. The ones who pause to stroke a cat or to pick up the

52

scattered treasures of the street: conkers, dropped pennies, the crumpled bunches of pink that fall from flowering cherry trees.

I do not know what it is like.

We were the people who did not stop and Sarah was the girl in the wheelchair.

Things began to change four or five years ago, one afternoon when Rose and Saffy and I were out with our father. We turned a corner and there were Sarah and her mother heading towards us. All at once, Rose (who was not quite five at the time) started bouncing about. She pointed to make us look, and she exclaimed in a very loud voice, 'Look! Look at the wheelchair girl!'

I can still remember how swiftly Sarah turned towards us, with her eyebrows raised and her eyes wide open and her face all ready to speak.

I wonder what she would have said.

Whenever I think of Sarah I see her with that look on her face.

I did not have more than a moment to look at Sarah because suddenly Rose and my father were having a battle on the pavement. My father had grabbed Rose's arm the instant she pointed. He hates rudeness and bad manners, and he was absolutely furious. He grabbed hard, and Rose did not like it. She kicked his legs. And so he picked her up and held her kicking in the air, and she hit his chest with her fists as hard as she could.

'Rose!' snapped my father. 'Stop it or I will smack you!'

Rose headbutted him and caught him just under his chin.

None of us have ever been smacked by our parents except Rose that one time. It was one smack and it was not hard – nothing like as hard as the headbutt had been. My father said afterwards that he was sorry, and Rose forgave him and fetched him a bit of soggy toilet roll to put on his bleeding lip.

'It was your fault,' she told him. 'I wouldn't have butted you if you had not said you would smack me.'

'I would not have said I would smack you if you had not hit me,' said my father.

'I would not have hit you if you had not picked me up.'

'But you were kicking me!'

'Because you grabbed my arm!'

'Because you were being so rude! Pointing like that at that girl! You *don't* point and you *don't* stare!'

'But she'd got a new hat just like my new hat!' wailed Rose.

★ ★ ★

54

If Rose had been allowed to run up to Sarah and say, 'You've got a new hat just like my new hat!' we would probably have made friends right then.

That walk with my father changed our relationship with Sarah, but it changed it the wrong way. It became worse. Saffy and I avoided looking at her completely. This was because we were embarrassed that she had seen our father smack Rose, no matter how gently. Even though his lip was bleeding and he had kick marks on his trousers.

Rose also stopped looking at Sarah. Instead, she stomped past her with her head down as if she was angry. Or ashamed. Or both.

Sarah put up with this treatment for ages. It was months and months before she lost patience and ran Saffron over with her wheelchair on purpose.

Soon after this, Saffron and Sarah became best friends, and they have been that way ever since. They bother about each other. For instance, if a combination of discos and wheelchairs and Valentine's Day happened to be making Sarah unhappy, then it would make Saffy unhappy too.

Tom used to say Sarah had witch's eyes. They are smoky, silvery, greeny-grey, and they show up so much because her skin is pale and her hair and eyebrows and eyelashes very dark. She is Saffron's age, so she is nearly two years older than me, but I am much taller. Tom used to say that Saffron was the most shattering-looking girl in the school, and that Sarah was the second most; but I would put it the other way around, and so would Rose.

'Do you think I will be shattering-looking when I am as old as Saffron and Sarah?' Rose asked once.

And Tom said, 'Good grief, I hope not, Permanent Rose!'

Sarah has been going to the same school as Saffron and me for not quite a year. Before that she went to the private school where her mother is the Head, but when Sarah and Saffron became friends she wanted to change. Sarah's mother said no, and she would not be persuaded to change her mind.

Then Sarah began her great campaign to escape. She hoped to be expelled, or at least asked to leave as soon as possible. She broke a private-school rule a day and made sure she was caught doing it. It was a very difficult time for her.

She stopped wearing school uniform. She stopped doing homework. She ate food in class – not just sweets, she took in sandwiches. She had pink and blue streaks put into her hair. She brought everything into school that was on the list of things not to be brought into school. She was always being sent out of class to get rid of gum or make-up.

Nothing worked.

Finally one day, she said to her mother, 'Tomorrow, because I can think of nothing else to do, I shall have to smoke in assembly.'

And then Sarah was allowed to leave at last.

Oscar the Mad Sixth-Former

All this happened ages ago. Sarah has been at the same school as Saffron and me for more than a year now. There was a Valentine's disco last February, of course; Saffron went, but somehow Sarah managed to avoid it.

David and I did the same, but even then I remember thinking that it might be easier to go. Then at least you would not continually have to explain why you were *not* going.

Peer pressure is an amazing thing. Sometimes it is like a storm-force wind. If you stand against it, you are liable to be flattened. That is why most people just let themselves be swept along.

Actually, this year I was quite happy to be swept along to the Valentine's disco, and I was sorry to hear that Sarah felt so bad about it.

Although I *completely* understood why.

There are discos at school several times a year, but the Valentine's Day disco is the one that everyone talks about. It is run by the sixth form, and they only sell the tickets in pairs. You have to ask someone, or be asked by someone, before you can go. Torture.

So I tracked down Oscar the mad sixth-former, who is organising it this year. He didn't take much tracking. He was in the library where he spends much of his time, keeping warm. (He says the wind-chill factor in the sixth-form common room has caused several cases of hypothermia, which the authorities have managed to hush up.)

'Why do we have to have this double ticket rule at the Valentine's disco?' I asked, after the customary polite greetings had been exchanged. (As Oscar would say.)

'Tradition,' said Oscar, stealthily concealing under the library table a suspicious-looking magazine.

'Change it,' I said.

'Why?' he asked. 'We had to suffer it in our time, so I don't see why you lot shouldn't.'

'It bothers a lot of people,' I said, and I was thinking of Saffron and Sarah and my friend David (who is desperate).

'What is your trouble, Indigo?' asked Oscar, grinning. 'Don't tell me you are having problems finding a girl!'

(As a matter of fact, I am not having problems finding a girl; but I did not tell him this.)

'Anyway, how the tickets are sold is the least of my worries,' he went on. 'You don't know what it is like organising this thing, mate. The school owns a very nice CD disco system with anti-shock players, two mikes and a mixer (not to mention two-hundred-watt speakers), but they have absolutely zero to play on it . . .'

(This is true. Our school's music collection is the accumulated left-over CDs from the last ten years of Christmas bazaars. Not so good, unless you are into Irish ballads. Or Sir Cliff. In which case, lucky you. Prepare to be blown away.)

'And then there is the lighting,' continued Oscar, who had obviously been in need of a good moan, and was well launched now. 'No strobes, in case someone has a fit; no dark corners . . . Dear, oh dear, stop sniggering, Indigo! Or was it a rueful smile?'

'I could not say,' I told him. 'I did not see it.'

He aimed an unenthusiastic swipe at the top of my head (which is higher than his) and carried on with the big moan.

'The drinks,' he said. 'You would not believe it! Nothing bright blue or orange (additives). Nothing in glass (well, fair enough, I am all for minimising loss of blood). Also nothing in cans because the little devils shake them up and squirt them . . .'

Oscar fell silent. Brooding. I thought it was the end, but there was more to come.

'The clearing up afterwards,' he said sadly, shaking his head. 'Oh yes. Someone has to do it. And someone has to nag the PE staff into being stewards – their first aid training is an asset, that's why we target them in particular. They do not like it, but the Head puts on pressure. He holds the bi-yearly Australian school rugby tour over their heads like the sword of Damocles (a classical allusion which you need not pretend to understand).'

'Assume Cicero is a closed book to me,' I told him soothingly, 'and you will be very nearly right.'

Oscar sniggered (or was it a rueful smile?) and continued a bit more cheerfully. 'However, I have managed to delegate everything except the tickets and the music – and I don't mind the tickets (I get a masochistic thrill from that part, to tell the truth). It is the music that bothers me. It is trash every time, and the organisers get the blame.'

'Saffron told me it was rubbish last year,' I agreed.

'Oh did she?' he asked. 'Oh right. Oh dear. Saffron, your gorgeous sister. Yes. Well, what am I supposed to do about it? You must have seen the school's CD collection. It is the pits. And do you know where the music funds come from? The library budget. And do you know what the library budget is? Zero.'

'Borrow stuff,' I said.

'Who from?' he demanded. 'All my friends play rugby and listen to S Club 7. They download the chords of "Postman Pat" and learn to play it on their electric guitars. You wait until you get into the sixth form, mate. It is the jungle. That is why I have got stuck with this school disco job on my own. Mind you, I am not doing it out of kindness but because it will look good on my Oxbridge Uni application. I have nothing else to put down. Duke of Edinburgh and Boy Scouts and all that never worked for me. This disco is my sole use of personal initiative ever. Pity it is doomed from the start.'

'Yes it is,' I agreed.

Then Oscar gave me a very hard look and said, 'By the way, I hear you have a pretty good CD collection, Indigo!'

'But why don't you bring your own stuff?' I asked, ignoring both this big hint and the very hard look.

'My stuff!' he shouted. 'Are you serious? Do I look like a CD collector? I think not. I do vinyl, mate.'

Rose

When I told Rose about Oscar the mad sixth-former she said, 'He sounds like a prat!'

Rose was eating her supper at the time. It was a very large jam sandwich, and she was eating it in a spiral, going round and round the edge with little tiny bites, holding it up to her mouth with both hands, like a hamster.

'A prat,' she repeated, looking at me over the top of her sandwich, and I could tell that this was the first time she had used that particular word and she was waiting to see what I would do.

My father says when Rose uses offensive language, it is simply attention-seeking. We should ignore her, he says, and eventually she will get tired of it and stop.

It is all very well for him; he lives in London and does not have to listen.

So I said, 'Actually he is very nice indeed and

anyway, I'm off, if you are going to talk like that.'

Then I left her (dripping jam all over the table) and went upstairs to my bedroom. Sure enough, two minutes later, she was bashing on the door and shouting, 'OK, I won't say it again. Let me in!'

'Wash the jam off, too,' I told her, without opening the door.

'How do . . . ?' I heard, and then I heard her tiptoe away and there was the sound of very quiet, secret washing in the bathroom.

'Why doesn't Oscar like CDs?' she asked, coming in very damp and polite, as if nothing had happened. 'What is the matter with them? You have millions, and so does Tom. I saw them when I was in America.'

(Rose is very proud of having been to America. She got there by emotionally blackmailing my father.) (And why not?)

Actually, I do not have millions of CDs, but I have a lot. I bet I have the best music collection in our school anyway. Most of it comes from Tom. He burns me copies of his own CDs. They are everything from classic rock to last week's number one in America. He sends them over by the dozen. Now and then I take a couple into school. They always draw a crowd of people asking, 'Where can I get that?'

'You can't,' I tell them. 'It's all about who you know.'

I don't lend them to anyone either. I just let them hear enough to know what they are missing.

'Start giving anything away,' Tom says, 'and sure as you know it, sooner or later the weirdos will show up.'

Tom spent a whole term at our school, so he knows what he is talking about. There are a fair amount of weirdos in this place, and most of them had a go at Tom and me in the past.

How times change.

Thank goodness.

Rose loves the music that Tom sends over. She said, 'You could do a disco with the best music in the world if you wanted to.'

'Yes, I could,' I said. 'If I wanted to.'

'Everyone would think it was fabulous,' said Rose.

Times may have changed, but I have not forgotten. I am not all that eager to make life fabulous for the weirdos yet.

'But maybe there wouldn't be much point in doing it,' continued Rose, 'because Sarah says she and Saffy aren't going.' And she looked at me just the way she had looked at me earlier, over the top of her jam sandwich. Trying me out.

'Maybe you should be going to bed,' I said.

Rose had the brains to change the subject at once.

'Did you know I found someone for every single

one of those Valentine's cards I made?' she asked.

'No. But I am glad to hear it. They were fantastic.'

'I wonder if Derek will ever get his,' she said thoughtfully.

'I shouldn't think it is very likely,' I told her, because it is no good patronising Rose. She is not silly. And there was very little hope that her card to Derek (which she posted last night with a second-class English stamp) would ever reach him, because it was addressed to:

Derek with the Bus
Tangier

Which, even if there is only one Derek in Tangier (unlikely) and only one bus (no hope there at all), would be still expecting a lot of the North African post.

'Anyway, I sent it,' said Rose, peacefully. 'That's what matters. Whether he gets it or not. Tom will get his, I know, because I put eight stamps on and I wrote the address twice on both sides. In big writing and little writing. Do you think he will like it?'

Once, when Tom was over here, to tease Rose I asked him, 'Before she was born, can you remember? Were things just the same as they are these days? Did it still rain and get dark, and all the stuff it does now? Did the sun go up and down in exactly the same way?'

'Yes,' said Tom, and then he smiled at Rose and said, 'No. Not really. Not exactly the same way.'

So I think he probably will like her card.

This Is How I Do Special
(Part 2)

My sister Saffron had a horrible time at the Valentine's Day disco last year. She was too fussy. Everyone who asked her she turned down, waiting for the right person to turn up and sweep her away. Which did not happen – he was otherwise engaged (dusting his vinyl). And when at last it became apparent to her that she was going to have to settle for a lesser being, there was nearly no one left. And the one she ended up with shut her head in a fire door and was sick on the dance floor and finally nicked her money and disappeared. It is very surprising that she noticed how bad the music was, all things considered.

I explained this to my good friend David, who has been asking me since Christmas to get her to go with him. It cheered him up a lot. David is blond-haired and always a bit out of puff. He is scared of girls, and he has no illusions about his ability to charm, but he knew he could do better than that.

'Tell Saffy,' he said, 'that I will not shut her head in a fire door or get sick or nick her money.'

'Tell her yourself,' I said – but he daren't. He once saw Saffron without any clothes on and he has never got over it. Poor David. (Although if he is going to start asking girls out he would do better to start with someone easier than Saffy.) (Not that it is ever any good telling someone who they should, or should not, go out with. I have learned this from living with my sister Caddy. You could subtly guide her judgement, by saying, for example, '*Your* boyfriend patted *my* bum,' but that was the most you could do. And it hardly ever worked.)

Anyway, Saffy says she isn't going to the Valentine's disco, and I cannot see an invitation from David persuading her to change her mind.

'Last year was the most humiliating night of my life,' said Saffron. 'And painful. And expensive.'

'Well, it's probably a good job it was,' said Rose, tactlessly. 'You will be able to stay at home with poor Sarah. She couldn't go anyway.'

'Oh, and why not?' demanded Saffron, because she hates anyone saying Sarah cannot do anything.

'What would be the point?' asked Rose. 'She would have to sit and watch all the time and know everyone was being sorry for her. She would hate that. What could Sarah do at a disco?'

'Dance,' said Saffron furiously, and she went out, slamming the door.

'She's in a mood,' said Rose. 'She is fed up. So is Sarah. So is David. So are you. So is everyone except me.'

Rose was right. She was the only one of us not fed up.

Rose is not scared of what people think. She made twenty Valentine's cards, and found someone to send every one of them to, and I bet they will all be pleased.

'Why *did* you send Valentine's cards to all those people,' I asked her, as she was going up to bed that night.

'Well, I couldn't send them all to Tom, could I?' asked Rose.

I remembered then the night when she made them. She did them all so carefully, and she said, as she finished the last one, 'They are all for Tom, really.'

I was beginning to understand a bit more the way that Rose did special.

What I did not understand was that sometimes *only*

special is good enough. I found this out the next day, when I asked Sarah if she would come to the disco with me.

Sarah said, 'Indigo! One, I have known you ever since you were a ten-year-old wimp afraid of falling out of your bedroom window. Two, me and Saffron are not going anyway (and, as well, Saffron says the music will be rubbish). Three, I have a wheelchair, as you must have noticed.'

When she had gone, Rose, who had been listening at the door, said, 'That was a definite No.'

But why? Why was it a definite No?

I asked Rose this question. There was no one else to ask.

Rose said it was like one Valentine's card.

'Don't you remember?' asked Rose. 'One, she wouldn't open. Patronising, she said. Ten would be a set-up. But she would have to open twenty. She said.'

Twenty Valentine's cards was how Rose did special.

I had to find a way to do special myself.

Oscar the mad sixth-former said, 'Nobody could dance to half this stuff.'

We were in the school library (again) and he was going through my CD collection. For someone who only does vinyl, he was taking a lot of interest.

'They couldn't dance to half of it,' he said, 'but otherwise it is fantastic.'

'You can borrow it and I will help you sort out a play list, if you put me in charge of ticket sales,' I said.

'No way,' he said.

So I started to repack the four large kit bags of CDs that I had carted to school that day.

After I had packed the first two he asked, 'Would your sister say the music was rubbish if we played this stuff?'

'No,' I told him, starting on the third. 'She would be dead impressed by your taste and acumen.'

'Acumen,' he repeated, and then he went over to the shelf where the dictionaries are kept and looked it up, while I packed my third bag.

'Oh would she?' he said, when he had found what it meant. 'My acumen? Oh that. Oh good.'

I did not pack the fourth bag straight away. I had a feeling a deal was coming after all.

'Oh well, why not?' he said. 'Let's go into partnership. My acumen and your music. You can sell the tickets if you like, but you have to turn over the cash to me every day to be locked up in the office. (It is destined for charity by the way, and the charity is the library budget – but keep that quiet as it is very unpopular. They wanted Donkey Rescue. I had to rig the vote.) And keep a list of everyone you sell to, because we will be checking at the door and if they are not on the list they will not get in. And mind you sell them in pairs,' he said, 'because we want equal numbers of all varieties and, besides, it is a tradition.'

So I agreed to all this, and I started my list, and the first people on it were me and Sarah.

'One,' I said to her, 'many years have passed since first we met. I can abseil out of my bedroom window with my eyes shut these days, no problem at all. Two, the music will be fantastic because I am supplying it. Three, I see no reason why you cannot leave your wheelchair to drape yourself on me during the slow dances, which are the only ones I am bothered about. Four, I have turned over my whole music collection to Oscar the mad sixth-former in order to impress you, and I cannot believe you are not bowled over. Also I have thought of a new system. Everyone who wants to go can give me their name and I will put them on my list and tell them who their partner will be. You are the first.'

'Gosh, you are stubborn,' said Sarah, laughing hard and unromantically.

Rose, listening at the door, came in and asked if that was a definite Yes.

'I suppose it's a definite Yes,' said Sarah.

★   ★   ★

I had to make a rule: No Complaining. People who complained about who I matched them up with were struck off. It would never have worked if I had allowed second choices.

My list was fantastic. It worked like magic. I wrote down the names, told them who their partners would be, and sold the tickets as fast as I could tear them out of the book. I paired football fans with football fans, dog lovers with dog walkers, and gigglers with dopes. I paired people by trainer brands, maths sets (i.e. brains), gruesome habits, and loudness of voice. I did it very very quickly, so no one had to wait around feeling unmatchable and rejected. I did not let anyone help.

I paired David with Saffron, and Saffron shouted a lot.

'Well, you weren't going to go at all,' I said. 'So what is your problem? It will save you choosing from the millions queuing up. And it is brilliant for David. He has very low self-esteem. Try not to think of it as a lifelong commitment.'

'Oh all right,' said Saffron. 'But only because I want to see what happens.'

Actually, I think a lot of people only came because they wanted to see what would happen, but I did not care. I had got my own way, and Sarah was coming with me, and she did not think I was patronising her either. She thought I was crazy.

'I am not crazy,' I told her, on Valentine's Day. 'This is how I do special.'

Appendices

This is all Rose's idea. I thought I had finished the story of the hugely successful (for some people) Valentine's Day disco, but Rose says not. She says I haven't said anything about:

1. Tom
Tom sent Rose a Valentine's card. It had a silver dragon on the front and a CD inside. Later we used the CD at the disco.

2. What happened to Oscar (and other people)
What happened to Oscar was that he got forgotten about until the very last minute, when I paired him up with Rose. Rose should not really have been there because she was much too young, but me and Sarah smuggled her in because she said it was not fair. During the course of the evening, Oscar and David swopped

partners. This did not upset Rose (who was only there for the pop), and was very nice for Saffron and Oscar, and I think David was secretly relieved although he did not say so. Rose taught David how to dance, and David taught Rose how to toss up marshmallows and catch them in her mouth, and whenever I caught sight of them they seemed to be enjoying themselves.

3. How my people-matching worked
On the whole my people-matching worked very badly. Surprise, surprise. The football fans were the worst of all because I took no account of who supported which teams. (I thought of it, but I couldn't be bothered.) Matching people by brains does not work either. Trainer brands was the biggest success. And dogs. Well, well.

4. Rose says I have not said anything at all about the slow dances.
You mind your own business about the slow dances, Rose. You were busy trying to catch marshmallows in your mouth. They were wasted on you.

WRITING, WHILE
ROSE WATCHES

by

Saffron Casson

Writing About Indigo's Disco While Rose Watches

I am writing this with a fountain pen on a block of unlined whitish-grey paper. The ink that I am using is black.

Rose has come to watch me write. This is something she often does. She likes to watch the letters flicking off the nib of the pen. It is something to do with the patterns they make, and something to do with the miniature movements of the pen, and something to do with the small rubbing sound of the nib on the paper. It is nothing to do with reading. I know she is not reading the words; she is just watching, in a sort of dream, and occasionally getting on with her own work.

If you could call it work. It just looks like nothing to me.

★   ★   ★

'Are you writing about Oscar?' Rose asked, when I had got this far.

'Why would I?' I asked.

'I would.'

'Oh.'

'Or Sarah.'

'Mmmm.'

'Or me. You could write about me.'

'Right.'

'I wouldn't mind.'

'I am writing about Indigo's disco,' I said (writing). (About Indigo's disco.)

When I looked up again, Rose had gone back into her dream.

Really I am writing about the star.

The balloon shaped like a star.

But I am starting with Indigo's disco.

I have read Indigo's account of the disco he organised, and I have noticed that it ends on a self-congratulating high with the lights going up at the end of the evening.

More could be said, but Indigo does not bother.

In particular, my enigmatic little brother does not mention that the next big social event after the Valentine's Day disco was the Valentine's Day flu.

It struck like a medieval plague. Within forty-eight

hours of the lights going up, half the school had collapsed.

There are not as many seriously thick people in our school as Indigo and the last set of government inspectors to beam down from the rose-coloured planet would have everyone believe. (Indigo's judgement was damaged in his first gruesome term, while the school inspectors were completely outwitted by our dramatic and improvisational skills. By day three they were reduced to handing out free tissues. But I digress.) Of course it was realised that the timing of the plague was no coincidence. The disco had become known as Indigo Casson's Disco. The new illness was swiftly attributed to the same hero: Indigo Casson's Bug.

People are weird. ICB became a measure of social success. If you were down with it, it was taken to mean that you had had a pretty good time at the disco. If you escaped, you hadn't.

Rose was very pleased with the neatness of this logic, although I told her that it was rubbish.

'Look at Indigo and Sarah,' she argued. (Those two had been among the first to fall.) 'Proof!'

'Look at you and David,' I said in reply. 'Explain that!' And I thought that I had won, because David (with whom Rose had spent most of the evening) was ill, and Rose was not.

However, Rose explained it perfectly easily. She said the reason that she had escaped, while David (to his great pride and delight) had been diagnosed a health hazard, was simple. The two of them had spent a happy time seeing how well they could catch marshmallows in their mouths. Rose had refused to eat the ones that fell on the floor; David hadn't.

'It must be one of those diseases you can catch two ways,' said Rose. 'Eating off the floor. Or snogging.'

Then she look at me very hard and added, 'You and Oscar didn't catch it.'

No, we didn't.

'I suppose,' went on Rose, continuing her very hard stare although it was getting no response from me, 'you and Oscar didn't eat stuff that fell on the floor . . .'

True. We refrained from that temptation.

'Or . . .' Rose paused, and she was just about to go one deduction too far and get herself into trouble when she was saved by the arrival of Eve.

'Darlings!' said Eve, dropping rolls of paper all over the floor and aiming kisses at both of us. Then she stooped to look at Rose's latest work of art. It was the side of a cardboard box. Rose was colouring it black.

'Goodness, Rosy Pose!' said Eve. 'More?'

Rose nodded.

'More black cardboard?'

'Yep.'

Lately, Rose's artistic output had consisted entirely of black cardboard. Eve looked at me with raised eyebrows, asking if I knew why. I shook my head. I didn't.

Rose noticed our exchange and explained, 'I need a lot of black cardboard.'

So that cleared up that mystery.

'No Oscar tonight then, Saffy?' asked Eve a few minutes later, after she had been upstairs to check on Indigo (who was sensibly having flu in bed with earphones on).

'Not tonight,' I said.

'I've been meaning to tell you how very much I like him.'

'I noticed on Saturday,' I told her.

Saturday was the day after the Valentine's disco. Oscar and I were in town together, and while we were there we accidentally bumped into Rose and Eve. I would have dodged this meeting if I could, but they saw us before we saw them.

I was not very happy as Eve and Rose came calling

and waving up to Oscar and me; I couldn't help wondering which of the three of them would disgrace me first.

I need not have worried. They all behaved beautifully. Rose said, 'Thank you for letting me come to the disco last night.' Oscar took off one of his hats (he wears two: a peaked one with earflaps, over a blue knitted beanie with snowflakes) and shook hands with both of them. Eve, in a valiant attempt at domestic normality, invited him to our house for Sunday lunch.

Eve loathes cooking and usually leaves Sunday lunch to: 1) Bill, 2) Indigo, 3) Fate (in order of availability); so no wonder she was visibly enchanted when Oscar told her that he never ate lunch.

'Darling!' she exclaimed so approvingly that Oscar went on to explain that not only did he not eat lunch, but also he did not eat breakfast, dinner or supper.

'Or tea?' asked Rose.

'Or tea,' agreed Oscar, and added (complacently) that he was therefore impossible to cook for.

Eve's ideal person is impossible to cook for, although Rose's is not. Rose looked at Oscar with wide, astonished eyes and exclaimed, 'But everyone eats!'

'Yes, of course everyone eats!' agreed Oscar.

'Well then!'

'I just (you know what I mean) think it's weird they

sit down and do it. Plates and tables and not letting stuff get cold . . . All that . . . Crazy!'

'Crazy!' repeated Rose.

'Yes, crazy!' said Oscar, and pulled his second hat back on again while Rose and Eve both nodded – Eve enthusiastically and Rose resignedly (after all, it was not the first time she had heard this point of view).

So that was how Oscar acquired Eve as a fan.

'Yes,' she said remembering, as she began smashing eggs and stirring them up in a bowl (she was about to attempt to make an omelette). 'I did like Oscar! Utterly charming! His lucky, lucky mother!'

Rose, who had paused her colouring to watch Eve's ambitious manoeuvres with the eggs, now stated very forcefully that: 1) she could not bear crunchy omelettes and 2) it was a pity that her sisters could not have normal boyfriends, like everyone else's sisters did.

Then her pencil-point snapped off, and she growled.

'Oscar!' she said crossly, gnawing herself a new point with her teeth. 'No one is called Oscar in real life!'

'Didn't you like him, then?' asked Eve, scooping in her bowl for bits of shell.

Rose picked splinters of wood from her tongue and looked thoughtful. I could see her weighing up the facts: He let me go to the Big School disco vs. He doesn't eat meals.

Eventually, after Eve and I had waited for a long long time, she said, 'He had nice green eyes.'

'What about the rest of him?' asked Eve, laughing.

'I didn't see the rest of him,' said Rose.

Watching Your Best Friend
With Not Enough Oxygen

Sarah was not ill the way the rest of Indigo's victims were ill. She was much, much worse. The flu restarted the illness she had had when she was little. Her damaged joints swelled; her bones and muscles hurt; she had pain in her chest, and fever. Not that Sarah told me any of this; I had it (in gruesome detail) from her mother, Mrs Warbeck. (Mrs Warbeck tells me to call-her-Liz, but I cannot do it. I don't know why.)

For three days I was not allowed to visit Sarah, but I telephoned every day. At first the news was almost entirely medical: a list of symptoms chanted by Sarah's mother, like something she had learned by heart. Often, in the background, I heard a sort of feeble groaning counterpoint by Sarah of: 'Saffy, don't listen! Mum, shut up!' (I obeyed; Sarah's mother didn't.)

However, as Sarah's mother became more resigned

to the facts (Sarah Is Ill), the theme of the chant changed. Now I was told how Sarah was the worst patient in the world, alternating between motionless non-communication and endlessly repeating that she was bored, that it was possible to die of boredom, that poor zoo animals *did* die of boredom, and that she, Sarah, knew how they felt. (The counterpoint of 'Saffy, don't listen! Mum, shut up!' did not change, but there was an addition: 'I am much better. When is Saffy coming? I am much better. Ask Saffy if she will come.'

'She isn't much better,' said Sarah's mother. 'She is worn out.'

'Ask Saffy,' said a voice, very faintly.

Sarah may have been worn out, but her mother was worn down. On the fourth day she called me and said, 'Saffy. Saffy dear, I have been thinking. Perhaps you could pop over now and then? Not to stay, of course. Just, for example, five minutes at a time. Or even less. Five minutes at the most, shall we agree? To say a word or two. No big chats (of course). I shouldn't like to have to . . . Well, I know I can trust you not to be – silly.'

It was about as unwelcoming invitation as I have ever had. But Sarah is my best friend, so I began visiting at once – for five minutes at a time (as instructed), two or three times a day.

Sarah's mother did not trust me one bit. Each time she opened the door and said, 'Oh Saffy, how lovely!' I could see her bracing herself. Part of me wanted to say, 'It was your idea! You asked me to come!' I didn't, because in real life Sarah's mother is very nice. I understood that, to her, these days were not real life.

Sarah looked awful but I did not mention it. She was desperate for news of the outside world. 'Tell me about everyone,' she ordered, so I told her about Indigo, voluntarily exiled in his bedroom with flu and the Internet for company, and Rose and David and the marshmallows, and Caddy and her new boyfriend.

'And what about you and Oscar?' Sarah demanded. 'The multi-layered Oscar. How is he? Cool, or just very, very cold?'

This was a reference to the fact that Oscar wears many of his clothes in twos. Two T-shirts (one short-sleeved, one long); two tops (woolly jumper under padded jacket); and of course, two hats. Not to mention the long black scarf he drapes around his neck when he is in danger of being exposed to severe climatic dangers (like air-conditioning).

'All that padding is suspicious,' said Sarah. 'Either he is concealing something or he feels he needs to be seen as impenetrable. Why else would anyone wear all their clothes at once?'

'I don't know,' I admitted. 'But I have to tell you that I may have discovered the only person in the world who can look good eating popcorn with fingerless gloves.'

'And when was this?'

'Last night at the cinema.'

'Go on! Huge progress!'

'Not huge,' I said, 'because it was a terrible Japanese film with subtitles. You know, the ones they show on Wednesdays that nobody ever saw the first time round?'

'Classics,' said Sarah wisely.

'And there were only six people there besides us, and we were the youngest by about fifty years . . .'

Sarah started grinning.

'And the only non-Japanese . . .'

'Oh Saffy!'

'And the only ones who brought in popcorn.'

Then we laughed until Sarah's mother called upstairs, 'Sarah, your chest!'

Which stopped us.

The next day I had a phone call from Sarah's mother saying, 'Perhaps Sarah should have a quiet day today,

Saffy, do you think? She had a very bad night. I wonder if she did too much yesterday?'

I said that, as far as I knew, Sarah had done nothing at all yesterday except lie in bed.

'All the same,' said her mother. 'I'll give her your love, shall I?'

Then in the background I heard, 'Saffy, don't listen! Mum, shut up!'

So later on that day I pretended I thought I had left my mobile there, and went round anyway. Mrs Silver, the cleaning lady, opened the door, and I sneaked upstairs without anyone else knowing I was there.

'Are you really too poorly for me to come?' I asked.

'Course not,' said Sarah. She did not say anything for a while after that, and then she said, 'I'm fine.'

'Good.'

'Will you come again soon?'

'If you like.'

'Just to check I am not dead,' she said. And then she opened her eyes and saw the expression on my face, and explained, 'Mum is too emotionally involved to be a reliable source of info and so (alas) am I.'

'Alas' is a very reassuring word, I think. Hearing Sarah work it into a sentence so neatly made me feel much happier. I looked round the room for something cheerful to talk about.

'Do you remember the night we put Rose to bed in the hammock?'

Sarah shook her head.

'You must. She had locked herself out in a thunderstorm when she went to rescue Eve from the lightning in the shed.'

'Did she?'

'Can I have your life-size model of lovely Justin?' I asked (thoroughly alarmed). 'Rose is in need of black cardboard.'

'No,' said Sarah, sitting up a bit. 'I am nothing like as ill as that yet.'

But the next day even I could tell that she was. She said, 'Take anything and go away.' Then she lay still and closed her eyes.

I went home and worried and worried until her mother telephoned and said, 'Sarah has asked me to ask you what you took.'

The worse Sarah felt, the better her jokes became. It was like a battle. Sickness vs. Jokes. The battleground was Sarah.

I understood this and I joined in on her side. Sarah's mother did not understand. She thought that Sarah was being flippant, when really she was fighting.

★ ★ ★

'If one day you come and find me not moving,' said Sarah, the next day, 'there is a Swiss army knife in the top drawer of the desk in the hall. Promise me you will open up a vein.'

I moaned a bit and said I did not see what good it would do.

'Saffy, use your brains!' said Sarah. 'It is how they tell if you are dead. No blood means it's over.'

'I am sure there are less messy ways of telling if you are dead,' I said, 'and anyway, it is two flights of stairs down to your hall. It is asking a bit much.'

'Forget it then,' whispered Sarah. And then after a while she added, 'I have a terrible fear of being buried alive.'

She looked so forlorn that I had not even the heart to say, 'Who hasn't?' And although I had promised nothing, I tiptoed out of the room.

'Any vein in particular?' I asked, when I crept back in.

She turned her head a little on the pillow in a hopeless kind of way, but I saw a glint under her quivering eyelashes.

'OK then, left wrist,' I announced, and I was just getting out the bottle-opener attachment when Sarah's mother came in.

Some things you do are impossible to explain. This was one of them. Sarah's mother said, 'I am shocked. Shocked.'

'Lighten up, poor old Mum,' said Sarah. 'I was in no danger. Saffron is rubbish at practical biology. Seriously, she is.'

'Seriously!' said Sarah's mother. 'Seriously! I don't think you know anything about seriously!'

'She doesn't like us laughing,' I told Rose when I got home.

'I thought it was supposed to be good for people,' said Rose. 'Laughing.'

So did I.

Sarah was very pleased when I reappeared the next day. She looked more like herself than she had for ages (the bottle-opener treatment must have worked after all), she was just out of the shower and was in her dressing gown, drying her hair.

'Wasn't it a long night, Saffy?' she said. 'I kept thinking: Now it must be morning, and it never was. Was it a long night to you, too? What did you do after you left?'

'I went out with Oscar,' I said.

'Oh goody!' exclaimed Sarah. 'Out with the details,

and spare us nothing! Are you staying to listen, Mum?'

'Is that a hint?' asked Sarah's mother. 'Of course I am not staying! If you are getting dressed, put something warm on. Remember your chest!'

'My chest! My chest!' said Sarah. 'Would that there was more of it to remember! And yours is not much better, Saff. I sometimes wonder if either of us will ever feel the squeeze of a 36C! What do you think, Mum?'

'I have more to worry about,' said Sarah's mother, primly. 'You both possess excellent brains (when you bother to use them). If you ask me, that is much more important.'

'Brains or boobs,' said Sarah sadly. 'I don't see why it has to be a choice.'

'Caddy has both,' I pointed out.

'So does poor old Mum,' said Sarah. 'Mind you, look where it's got her!'

This remark caused Sarah's mother to march out of the room, but she marched out smiling. Things were getting much better.

Sarah curled up on her bed and started examining her face in a mirror.

Her mother stayed downstairs and vacuumed.

I described my night out with Oscar, which had begun with a telephone call to my house.

★ ★ ★

'Is that you, Saffy?' he asked, when I picked up the phone.

'Of course it is!' I said.

'What are you doing right now?'

'Nothing,' I said, and Caddy, who was home for the night, shook her head violently at me and mouthed: 'Much too honest!'

'Oh good,' said Oscar. 'I'm on my way then. Wear lots of clothes.'

This unusual-for-a-new-boyfriend advice should have alerted me, but it didn't. I was so alarmed at the thought that he would be round any minute, that it hardly registered. I began running around in panicking circles saying, 'Have you got to have that stupid video on again, Rose? I don't know why we had to have curried eggs tonight of all nights. This house smells like a curried drain and there's eggshells all over the kitchen and why are you wearing pyjamas, Eve? It's not even seven o'clock, it looks weird. And I don't see why every time Caddy comes home we have to have ten weeks' worth of knickers drying on the radiators.'

Nobody took any notice at all except Rose, who turned *Mr Bean* up even louder, and Caddy, who said calmly, 'Meet him on the doorstep. That's what I always did.'

I remembered then how Caddy used to vanish from

the doorstep – one moment there, the next gone, as if snatched by aliens into another world. (She would reappear, sometimes what seemed like days later, looking thoughtful.)

Now it was my turn on the doorstep – and very soon, there I was, shivering in Caddy's new jacket with her mobile, freshly charged, in my bag.

'Ring if you need rescuing!' she instructed. (What had happened, during those alien kidnappings?) 'Where are you going, anyway?'

That was what I had forgotten to ask. But ten minutes later, nearly frozen solid, I found out.

'Hi Saff!' said Oscar, looming suddenly up through the darkness and kissing me with more accuracy than is usual in my experience. 'Come on! Hurry! It won't last for ever! They'll have a back-up generator, they always do.'

'Who always do?' I asked stupidly.

'St Matthew's at the top of the hill,' he said. 'The power is off and their floodlighting has failed. It will be fantastically dark in the graveyard tonight.'

I looked across at Sarah to see a new expression on her face; one I had never seen before: stunned disbelief. She saw me looking, became aware of it herself and smoothed it away, all in an instant.

'So was it?' she asked sweetly. 'Dark?'

'Yes,' I told her. 'It was.'

However hard Sarah tried, she could not quite get rid of that expression. Every time she wiped it away, it reappeared again.

'Stars,' I said, 'that is what it was all about. Stars.'

'Stars,' repeated Sarah, looking stupid.

And then I suddenly remembered something. The exact prop I needed.

Nearly every day someone or other in my family has sent something to Sarah to cheer her up. It was Rose who had started this idea, and Rose who had pestered people until they made an effort and joined in (she had even forced Bill to send pink carnations from London). I had the job of delivering these offerings, and I generally left them outside the door. 'Until the opportune moment,' as Sarah put it.

I hurried out of the room to fetch the latest.

The last time, it had been from Rose. She had taken a break from colouring black card to draw a picture of Indigo, decorated with real hair – cut from him while he slept.

This time it was a gift from Eve, and one I had nearly refused to deliver: a fat, star-shaped helium balloon that she had bought the day before from a market stall.

As soon as I had seen it, I had known I did not like

that balloon. I had been glad that it was too late in the day to take it round to Sarah. I had put it away out of sight, and then Oscar appeared and swept me off the doorstep and into the unknown blackness of St Matthew's. So I forgot about the balloon until late in the night.

That was when I awoke suddenly with the cold feeling of being watched. As if there was someone in the dark room standing over me, someone I would see when I opened my eyes.

Rose, I thought at first. Rose often has bad dreams. Sometimes she does come searching for one of us to comfort her in the night.

But Rose would have had to open the door, and I would have heard that. Rose would not have waited in silence for me to wake up. She would have pushed into bed with me, begging, 'Saffy, move up!'

My door had not opened, and the pale face leaning over to watch me in the dark was not Rose.

Of course, it was the balloon, somehow escaped from the wardrobe where I had stowed it earlier that evening.

I knew it was ridiculous to be scared of a balloon, but all the same I could not bear to have it in the room with me. I got up and took it downstairs.

I don't think it stayed there for very long.

The little *scritch-scratch* noise outside my bedroom door that haunted me until morning was the sound of it bobbing against the ceiling there.

It had soon found its way back to me again . . .

In the morning I told Oscar that the balloon was too silly to take to Sarah. It really *was* silly too; Eve had bought it in a great hurry. She had hardly noticed that on one side there were pale-pink letters announcing:

A silver star to light your way

and she had not seen the other side at all until she got it home, when she turned it over and was surprised to find that the announcement continued:

Baby daughter born today!

Which even I had to admit was funny.

Oscar would not hear of me not taking the balloon. 'It's very important that Sarah should see it,' he told me. 'It's a symbol of the decaying and debased nature of Western Art. Anyway, it will make her laugh.

'It's perfect, Saff!' said Oscar.

Up in Sarah's bedroom, with that expression of stunned disbelief coming and going on her face, it suddenly seemed perfect to me too.

'Stars!' I repeated, putting the balloon's silver ribbon

into Sarah's hand. 'Those white dots in the sky! That's why the churchyard was so good in the dark! That's what we did, for hours and hours! He knows all their names! I have never been so cold!'

Then suddenly Sarah understood, and she started grinning. And when she saw what was written on her own star, she began to laugh. She laughed until tears poured down her cheeks. The balloon escaped because she was laughing so much that she could not hold the ribbon. *Scritch-scratch*, it went, rocking comically against the ceiling, and Sarah laughed and laughed.

Oscar had said it would make her laugh.

Sarah laughed until she could not stop. Every time she caught sight of the silver balloon she laughed still more. She laughed until she coughed. She laughed until she could not prop herself up. She laughed until she choked. She laughed until her breathing changed to gasping, dragging, wheezing gulps for air.

Asthma.

The balloon still rocked gleefully against the ceiling, but I stopped laughing.

Then Sarah's mother came running into the room, and she saw me, and she saw Sarah.

'SARAH!' she shouted. 'Saffron! Come here and help me!'

But I did not help her. I grabbed the balloon and I

pulled the window open, and I pushed the balloon outside.

It went up and up, triumphant into the dusky blue-grey evening sky, rocking and nodding like a thing alive. And I ran across the room and down the stairs and out of the door and away down the road.

I ran away as fast as I could.

I did not stay to help.

It was not just my fault. Who made me take that balloon to Sarah's anyway? Oscar. And who started all this take-something-to-Sarah-every-day stuff? Rose. And who bought the horrible stupid balloon in the first place? Eve.

And Sarah's mother never said one word about asthma.

Or did she?

What about all those phone calls when I did not listen?

Yes, well, who said, 'Saffy, don't listen!'

Sarah.

This is not the first time Sarah has got me into trouble.

It is not fair. Nobody will remember the hundreds and hundreds of times I have been there for Sarah. They will just remember the one time I ran away.

Anyway, Sarah is all right now; her mother rang to say that. She left a message with Eve. 'Saffron will probably be relieved to know that Sarah is very much better.'

Nothing will ever be the same again.

She was a very inconvenient friend to have anyway.

Change the Subject (Part 1)

When I have had enough of Rose asking me questions that are none of her business I say, 'Change the subject.'

Rose said, 'Me and Indigo wondered if you had quarrelled with Sarah.'

'Oh did you?'

'So we rang her up and asked and she said, "Don't be stupid".'

'So, *don't* be stupid!' I said. 'And change the subject! Why *are* you colouring all that cardboard black?'

'I am going to stick it all together when I have got enough,' said Rose, 'and make a fold-up sky.'

'A fold-up *black* sky?'

'Yes.'

'No stars? No moon? No clouds? No aeroplanes? No lights? No comets? No fireworks? Nothing?'

'No.'

'Just plain black?'

'The sky is sometimes just plain black,' said Rose.

Well, that's true.

Change the Subject
(Part 2)

'What are you writing now?' asked Rose

'I am writing about Oscar's car,' I told her.

'The Icon,' said Rose.

'That's right. The Icon.'

Oscar did not have an eighteenth birthday party. Nor did he have any presents. He had money instead. He said most of his relations had no problem with that.

'They have not got what it takes to choose the gear for me,' he said. 'And they have realised it at last, which is nicer all round. (It miffs the grannies no end to find their offerings have been flogged on eBay, but what can you do?)'

'What?' asked Rose, who had been listening with fascination to these graceless remarks.

'That's what I've come to show you,' said Oscar, and led us outside.

It was the most hideous car that I had ever seen, bright green, with googly eyes for headlights and a warty plastic roof. It looked like a giant toad. An ancient, unhappy, giant toad.

'There!' said Oscar, smirking.

'What is it?' I asked.

'It is an Icon!' said Oscar. 'They don't make them like that any more. It is a Classic. It is French design at its Ultimate. It is a Modern Antique. I bought it off the Internet with the birthday takings. What do you think?'

Rose and I looked at each other, and we both understood without a word that this was not the moment to say what we thought. It would have been too unkind. However, while I was searching for a few tactful words of admiration, Rose asked: 'Does it go?'

'Go?' repeated Oscar. 'What d'you mean, does it go? How do you think I got it here? It goes like a dream. Ride in that and you are riding in history. The earth moves. Wild!'

'I don't see how,' said Rose.

'Well, get in and I'll show you,' said Oscar.

That was how Rose and I ended up stranded in a lay-by high up on the road that crosses the moors to the east of the town. It was mid-afternoon in a landscape that was sodden, freezing, dark and probably haunted.

Oscar had been very depressed when the Icon (and therefore the earth) ceased to move.

'It didn't do anything like this before,' he said.

The Icon had ground more and more slowly up the long, long hill. Then it had coughed in a hopeless kind of way. Then it had drifted into the side of the road. Then it had died.

A waiting silence filled the car: the sort of silence that occurs when a miracle is (hopefully) imminent.

'Well,' said Oscar, when no miracle had occurred. 'Better take a look.'

He paused for a moment, probably hoping Rose and I would say, 'Do not sacrifice yourself so rashly!' because you could tell by the way the sheep were standing that it was definitely chilly outside.

But we didn't. So poor Captain Oates (Oscar) pulled down the earflaps of number two hat, wound a few extra loops of scarf around his neck, climbed out, raised the Icon's rusty bonnet and peered inside.

'Nothing wrong there!' he announced, about two seconds later.

Rose, who had scrambled out after him, came to peer too.

'What would it look like if there was?' she asked.

'Obviously,' said Oscar, 'well, obviously, there would be, you know . . .'

'Smoke?' suggested Rose helpfully.

'Maybe.'

'And broken wires?'

'Could be.'

'And holes with stuff coming out?'

'Yes,' agreed Oscar, clearly relieved to have the technical details so confidently provided. 'That sort of thing.'

Then they both looked back inside again and shook their heads and said, '*Definitely* nothing wrong there.'

Having settled that worry for certain, Oscar climbed back into the car and folded me in his arms. (A gesture not of attraction, but of refrigeration, as I realised when he unfolded me and remarked with obvious disappointment, 'You're not very warm, either.')

What will I do without Sarah to share these things with? No one appreciates ludicrous detail as much as she. The more the better. (Change the subject.)

Rose had wandered off and begun jumping backwards and forwards over a small flooded ditch at the side of the road. Oscar was in a stupor (hypothermia). I, released from his chilly embrace, returned to what I had been doing ever since the non-arrival of the miracle, which was trying to remember where I had last seen my mobile phone.

Finally I remembered. In the kitchen, being recharged, and that's where it still was.

'I hope you have your mobile with you because I don't,' I said to Oscar.

'Actually Saff,' said Oscar, 'I'm between mobiles right now.'

Oh.

Rose's ditch-jumping was becoming more and more ambitious. She was working hard. She said afterwards she thought she might as well since it is no fun sitting in the back of a car while the people in the front are snogging.

How true.

But how inaccurate.

If Rose had looked, she would have seen that I was fuming and Oscar was not noticing. This went on for some time. Then I began rummaging through a black hole beside the steering wheel (French design at its Ultimate for a glove compartment) and Oscar lightened the atmosphere with a few merry musings on the Weather Forecast.

'Temperature's dropping,' he said. 'It will freeze

tonight. Or snow, if any clouds come up. This is always one of the first roads to get closed off— Whoops! There goes Rose!'

Rose had jumped once too often. A minute later she came hopping over to us and announced, 'I've got a wet foot.'

'It was going to happen,' said Oscar sympathetically, reaching back to open a door for her. 'Cold?'

Rose nodded, with chattering teeth.

Oscar took off his number two hat, turned round and pulled it carefully down over Rose's head. 'Twenty-five per cent of body heat is lost through the head,' he remarked. 'Don't ask me what happens to the rest of it because I've been trying all my life to find out and I still don't know. What's that you've got, Saffy?'

From among a sinister jumble of loose red and black wires (surely they should have been attached to something somewhere) I had just unearthed a very tatty car manual.

'The Book!' exclaimed Oscar joyfully when I held it up. 'The Book of Words! Excellent! Pass it over!'

I passed it over and it fell open at once at a very oily and well-thumbed section headed: Trouble-Shooting. The significance of this was lost on Oscar, who was already hopefully turning pages.

He did not stay hopeful for long. His page-turning

became slower and slower, and he muttered fragments of what he was reading aloud in so uncertain a voice that Rose asked from the back, 'Is it written in French?'

'Medieval English, more like,' answered Oscar. 'Starter motor disfunctionality? Pitting and fouling of ignition plugs? If you ask me this is a very bad translation . . . Distributor and timing . . .'

He gave a big sigh.

'With Mummy's car, it is always petrol,' Rose remarked.

Oscar swung round and gave Rose a very thoughtful look. Then he turned to the petrol gauge – the needle of which was pointing not just at FULL, but at some unknown register ever higher (BRIMMING, perhaps) – and gave it a hard slap.

The needle dropped at once to considerably less than ZERO. When Oscar slapped it again, it fell off completely.

'Superb!' he said, looking extremely happy. 'Fantastic! I knew there couldn't be anything wrong with the engine. I'll hitch into town and pick up some petrol and be right back. You two can stay here in the warm.'

Before we could even ask, 'What warm?' he was out of the car, blowing on his fingers and fastening buttons that most people do not know exist. He was about to walk off and leave us.

'How *can* you hitch into town?' I asked, jumping out after him. 'Only two cars have passed all the time we've been here.'

'So, I'll catch the third,' said Oscar. 'No problem.'

Then he really did leave us.

The long road that the Icon had climbed so slowly had led us far out of town, looping from side to side, higher and higher into countryside usually only seen on geography field trips. (Several ice ages, Oscar would not have been surprised to hear, had carved their traces on this landscape.) On either side of us were the broken lines of ancient dry-stone walls, little gullies like the one that Rose had jumped, running fast and clear with the accumulated rainwater of the winter, and miles and miles and miles of moor. Over everything was a purplish, brownish light. It made the outlines blurry, the faraway town a grey shadow, and the road a line sketched unreliably across the painted hills. Oscar disappeared around the first bend, and I climbed back into the car, and Rose said, 'I didn't know places could be spooky when it was still light.'

Before I could reply, a car came past, very fast, and then another, more slowly.

Two cars at home could pass unnoticed, every minute. It was amazing the disturbance that two cars caused in that solitary place: their noise, coming up on us out of the loops of road higher up the moor; the way their passing seemed to buffet the air around us; worst of all the way their daylight headlamps shone straight in our faces.

It was not nice.

Rose did not like it either. She looked at me round-eyed from under the brim of Oscar's hat and said, 'What if they had stopped?'

'Oh Rose, why would they?' I asked (although actually I could think of plenty of reasons). 'To steal this car? This is not the sort of car that anyone would want to steal.'

'Not to steal the car,' said Rose, and I could tell that she could think of plenty of reasons too, and that she was frightened.

'How long has Oscar been gone now?' she asked.

'About ten minutes.'

'What time is it?'

'A quarter to four.'

'Quarter to eleven in New York,' said Rose.

When Rose starts converting to New York time, it is a very bad sign. It means she has just about reached the limit of what she can bear.

'If I was in New York,' continued Rose, 'Tom would be there and it would be morning.'

I did not say anything.

'Do you like it here, Saffy?'

No, I do not like it here.

I tried to make myself be reasonable. I thought of all the books I had ever read where people end up in places like this. Old-fashioned story books, travel books, fantasy. They all had happy endings.

Unfortunately, Rose has read nothing except *Little Red Riding Hood*, and bits of *Morte D'Arthur*, both books whose plots rely very heavily on the omnipresence of murderous strangers.

As well as reading *Little Red Riding Hood* and *Morte D'Arthur*, Rose has listened to the news. From the back of the car I heard her give a quick gasp of dismay, and I looked round to see a white van coming up behind us.

'It is always white vans,' said Rose, and at the same time the sound of the van's engine slowed right down, and we knew that it had seen us. We turned our heads away, as if we did not care and were not alarmed, but still we knew that speculative eyes were staring in at us. It is possible to feel eyes. You do not have to see them to know they are there.

Whoever was driving that van slowed to a crawl.

I prayed: Please God do not let it stop, although I knew that this was ridiculous. I am not saying I do not believe in God, but I do not believe he hears all the prayers that must come hammering up twenty-four/seven from the frightened people of the Earth. If he does, he doesn't take much notice. You only have to look around to see that.

Rose did not pray. Rose used her brains. She reached across me, pushed open the door, and waved vigorously and hugely at an invisible presence just above us on the hillside. The van, which had been moving at walking pace, changed gear and moved suddenly away.

I jumped out of the car and ran and hugged Rose, who was pale and trembly and looking ready to cry.

'I don't like being nearly murdered,' she said.

'They might have been perfectly nice people, wondering if we needed help,' I argued. 'Or they might just have slowed down to look properly at the Icon.'

'Or they might have been murderers,' said Rose, 'getting all ready to jump out and grab. Until they saw me waving and thought someone was with us. What,' continued Rose, in a high, un-Rose-like voice, 'if they realise we were on our own and come back? It is always white vans. When people go missing, it always says on the news: Police Are Looking For A White Van. So.'

Once a thought like that is spoken aloud, it is no use trying to unthink it. Clearly there was no way that

Rose was going to get back into the car and wait quietly for Oscar. I did not blame her; I did not feel much like doing it myself. So I looked around for an alternative and found one almost straight away, a footpath leading up the hillside right beside the lay-by where we had come to rest. If we followed it for a few minutes we would soon be high enough above the road to see much further. We could look out for Oscar, plodding towards the town and see if he had managed to get a lift.

I suggested this to Rose.

There is no one I know who can go from utterly miserable to completely happy as fast as Rose. She exclaimed, 'Oh yes! Come on!' and began zooming up the path.

'As long as you won't be cold,' I said.

'I won't be cold,' promised Rose, whirling round and round. 'I've got this hat!' and she beamed up at me and patted it hard, showing me what a good hat it was, and her eyes were shining like stars.

Change the Subject
(Part 3)

Rose is no longer colouring squares of cardboard black. Just as I got used to it, she stopped.

After she stopped colouring her squares she began sticking them together, joining them with parcel tape on their non-black sides. She did this very carefully, first arranging the squares into lines, and then taping the lines together into blocks. When she turned the whole thing back over again, it looked just like a patchwork quilt. Every single square was a different shade of black. It covered nearly the whole of the living-room floor.

Rose was very, very pleased with it.

'It folds up just like I wanted it to do,' she said. 'And it unfolds just like I wanted it to do. And it is black as black all over.'

'That's OK then,' I said, and I went back to my writing. It was time to describe the moor.

★ ★ ★

The moor.

That was where we were, Rose and I, on a late February afternoon, with a clear sky and the lights of the town just beginning to show in the far distance.

How strange, I thought, how very strange, that we should be here on this cold moor. We had not chosen it, or talked of it, or planned it in any way, and yet it seemed the only place that we could be. We might have stepped into another life, so unconnected was it with anything to do with our own world.

That was what I imagined, looking around me, in that silent and empty place.

I know now that it is not that easy to step into another world. I thought it was, but I was wrong.

Rose was not doing any thinking at all. She was skitting and skipping up the path that led up a gradual slope to the nearby top of the hill. She went very quickly and lightly, in her little jacket and big hat, jumping the puddles along the way. I followed much more slowly because I had new trainers on and at that time I was still trying to keep them clean.

It was much, much further up to the top of the hill than it had looked from the road. Also there were cows. Not sheep. Cows. Cows with horns. They were far away, and they took no notice of us, but they were there.

That was our first problem.

The second was the footpath.

It had started off as a reasonable, clearly visible path; it had even been labelled: FOOTPATH. It did not stay that way for long. It became more and more narrow, the puddles more and more frequent, and the mud in between the puddles more and more difficult to avoid splashing on my feet. Rose was soon so far ahead that she was just a little grey figure under a hat, still skipping, still jumping puddles, and still happy. I knew that she was happy because she was singing her favourite song. Snatches of it came floating back down to me.

> '*I know a song that will get on your nerves*
> *Get on your nerves, get on your nerves*
> *I know a song that will . . .*'

Rose did not get many opportunities to sing this song uninterrupted; now she was making the most of them.

'Rose!' I yelled, cross with the song, and cross with the growing distance between us. 'Come back!'

> '*. . . get on your nerves! . . .*'

'Rose!'

I had reached a puddle too big for leaping, and had to pick my way through the tough boggy tussocks of grass round the edge.

'. . . I know a song . . .'

Another puddle: worse than a puddle, a winter stream seeping down across the path. Wet footprints on a couple of small and nearly submerged stepping stones showed how Rose had crossed. The second stone wobbled so much I nearly fell flat on my face. A clump of rushes saved me.

Where was Rose?

I stood still to listen properly.

'. . . that will get . . .'

There she was: that grey pixie silhouette, poised on a hillock of grass.

'. . . on your . . .'

'ROSE!' I roared.

'. . . nerves . . .'

Then there was a splash.

I gave up trying to save my trainers and started running, and found that it was easier than walking.

There was less time to sink at each footstep, that was why. It was no use pretending any longer that this was a path going up a hill. It was a bog, going round the side of a hill, and Rose was in the middle of it, and very soon I would be in the middle of it too.

'. . . *Get* . . .' (squelch) ' . . . *on your* . . .'
(squelch, squelch) '. . . *nerves* . . .'

She did not sound so happy now; quite disconsolate in fact, but much closer.

'Rose!'

Then I spotted her, just around a curve of hillside, clinging on to a clump of rushes, knee-deep in mud and water.

'Saffy!' she exclaimed in a suddenly-very-pleased voice when she saw me. 'I'm stuck!' And then she began again.

'. . . *get on your nerves, get on your nerves* . . .'

'Stop singing that awful song!' I ordered as I began picking my way towards her. 'And stand still! Why did you run so far in front?'

'. . . *get on your nerves* . . .'

'STOP IT!'

'I can't stop it,' said Rose. 'I've got it stuck in my

head. And I didn't run far in front, I just went a little way . . . *I know* . . . Sorry! Oh, Saffy!'

My left foot had suddenly plunged down way above my ankle. I yanked it out and leaped for the next tussock. It quivered like a jelly, and began to sink. I found one that was steadier, and then a bit of tough grass I could cling to. I was now quite close to Rose.

'Look at my trainers!' I said angrily, and balanced on one leg for a moment so that she could see the earthy black soup streaming from my left foot. 'Ruined!'

Rose, who knows the rarity of new trainers in our house, said, 'Poor Saffy,' half held out a tissue that she had fished from her jacket pocket, and then put it away again. 'Poor Saffy,' she repeated, humbly, and I had a sudden vision in my mind, as if from very far away, of Rose and me at that moment, me worrying about my trainers, and Rose, knee-deep in icy muddy water, worrying about them too. It made me ashamed.

'I know how you are supposed to get out of bogs,' said Rose, 'lie down and swim across the mud. But I don't want to. What are you doing?'

I had remembered that I was wearing a belt, and I was trying to get it off without over-balancing.

'How stuck actually are you?' I asked, cautiously testing the ground in between us.

'One leg not very and one leg quite a lot. Saffy! Don't get yourself stuck too!'

But I was not getting stuck. I had found a more solid bit of bog than the part I had crossed to get near Rose, and when I got my belt off and swung one end towards her she managed to reach it quite easily. Then I pulled and Rose pulled, and in a moment she was standing beside me, very muddy and shivery, but out.

We hugged each other in triumph, and then we discovered that my strongish bit of bog was in reach of another solidish part, and after that it was easy. The ground stopped dissolving under our feet and soon we were back on the heathery, grassy moorland again, with the bog behind us.

'I thought I would have to stay there while you fetched help,' remarked Rose, hugging herself and jumping up and down to warm up. 'Look at the lovely sunset shining in the puddles! What shall we do next, Saffy? Had we better go back?'

That thought was appalling. It was true that the puddles were pink and purple with sunset, but they would not be for long. The hillside was much darker now. All hope of reaching the top was over, and so was all chance of spotting Oscar on the road. However, beyond us but not very far ahead was a small cluster of buildings: a farm. Farms have roads, or tracks at least, and they have people and telephones. I explained all this to Rose as we watched the sunset fade from the puddles, and as the colours dimmed, so Rose's cheerfulness dimmed too. She did not want to go to the farm. She said, 'What if the people there are the white van people? What if it's their farm? We should go back the way we came till we get to the car. Oscar will probably be waiting there for us.'

'We would never find the way,' I argued. 'It is nearly dark, and freezing cold. Anyway, look how you sank.'

'Only up to my knees,' said Rose.

'And don't forget the cows.'

'They were only cows.'

'With horns. What if they ran at us?'

'Well,' said Rose. 'They would just be cows with horns running at us. And we would have to get out of the way, that's all.'

Poor Rose. She was more afraid of people in white vans than she was of being run at by cows with horns, or even re-crossing that miserable freezing bog in the dark. All the same, I made her come with me. It seemed the only thing to do.

The farm was two fields away, and then one.

There was something about that farm that was not right. Rose spotted it first, and since she had not wanted to go there in the first place, it pleased her very much.

'The farmer,' she said happily, 'is out! Good!'

'How do you know?'

'No lights in the windows.'

She was right, there were no lights in the windows. There were no lights anywhere.

'I can't see any animals either,' said Rose, looking round the fields nearby. 'Perhaps he's given them to another farmer to look after and gone on holiday.'

I felt like crying. A small ridiculous part of my brain had been remembering storybooks again, where farms meant farmers' wives full of friendly welcomes, hot drinks, warmth, and the immediate solution to all problems.

Well, of course, I had not really believed any of that, but I had thought we might get to a phone.

'I don't think it's a very nice farm at all,' observed Rose thoughtfully, as we got closer.

It was a horrible farm. The windows were black pits. The outbuildings were ruined and empty. Scrawny trees grew so close to the walls they half covered the broken doorway. The garden was a tangled waste of overgrown bushes and there were piles of sodden black junk everywhere. There were even the burnt-out remains of a rusty white van.

'Nobody has lived here for years and years,' I said.

And then we stood still for a long time, just looking, until Rose said very quietly, 'Saffy?'

'Mmmm?'

'Can you see something moving in the bushes, Saffy?'

'Oh, really, Rose! Oh, how silly!'

Yes I can.

Change the Subject
(Part 4)

Rose is flapping her black cardboard sky in my face and saying, 'Saffy! Look! Look up! Stop writing and look!'

'At what?' I ask.

'This. My sky. My sky isn't right.'

'What's the matter with it?'

'The back,' says Rose. 'Look at the back!'

It looks exactly as it always has to me.

'Is it coming unstuck?' I ask.

'No, no,' says Rose impatiently. 'Well, yes, a bit, but that's not it. I wanted it to look like a real black sky and it doesn't.'

(How true. It looks like black cardboard paving, but that is not what is bothering Rose.)

'It's wrong on the back,' she says.

'Wrong on the back?' I repeat (stupidly).

'Yes. On the back. On the other side. What colour do you think the real black sky is on the other side?'

'Black,' I say at once.

'Yes, black,' agrees Rose, and then she heaves hers over and spreads it out and we look at it. It is an unpleasant patchwork of cereal boxes, Christmas cards and junk mail adverts; all the different bits of card that she has used, held together with strips of brown parcel tape.

'That is not what the real sky looks like on the back,' says Rose, and I am forced to admit that she is probably right.

I wonder why Rose's art is always so large and messy and complicated.

I cannot think of any easy solution to this problem of the other side of the sky.

Rose does not seem to expect me to. I think she just wants me to understand that it's there, this unsatisfactory back to an otherwise pretty good sky. She folds it up again and begins, 'Sarah says—'

But I do not want to hear what Sarah says so I change the subject.

Something Moving in the Bushes

I should not want anyone to underestimate the nastiness of the place in which Rose and I now found ourselves to be. This was not some quiet spot where time had paused. It was not a place where nothing happened any more. There was a force hungry and moving on that farm. It was decay. Its marks were everywhere. You could look at the roof and watch it rot.

Do not forget that by now it was nearly dark.

That afternoon I realised something about darkness. It is stronger than light. Light can push the dark back, but it cannot get rid of it. The dark stays. It hangs about under leaves. It runs beside stone walls. It waits in doorways. When the sun goes down it leaks out of these places like a spreading stain.

There is nothing you can do about darkness when

you are out on a sodden moor in February without a torch. It comes, and you cannot stop it, and it engulfs you like water. Being able to see a light makes no difference at all, just as being able to see land far away makes no difference to the wetness of water.

Rose and I could see plenty of lights far away. There were car lights on the road, and clusters of lights on the dark hillsides that must be farms – proper farms, with telephones and people. There was a great luminous tangle of lights that was the town, so many they made an orange glow in the sky above.

But there were no lights here. And Rose was right. There was definitely something moving in the bushes.

'It's a face,' said Rose, her small frozen fingers pushing their way into my hand. 'It's Somebody.'

We had come up to the farm from one side, and until then all my attention had been on the buildings directly ahead of us, but now I understood the whole layout. The bushes were at the front of the house, between us and the track that clearly led away towards the road. We would have to pass them to reach it, and that meant we would have to pass whatever was moving amongst them. It was turned towards us, paler than any face I had ever seen.

'It's Somebody Horrible,' whimpered Rose, 'and they've seen us.'

There was no doubt about that, but it occurred to me that maybe they did not realise that we could see them. They were almost completely hidden in darkness. Only the paleness of their face betrayed their eagerness, as they dodged and ducked among the shadows.

'I want to go home,' sobbed Rose, tugging my hand. 'Come home, Saffy. Come away.'

But I could not come away. I could not move. There was something nightmarishly familiar about that twitching, jerking movement. I had seen it before. I took a step closer, and then another one.

And then I knew what the thing was that was moving in the bushes, and I knew why it was waiting there.

It was waiting for me.

How many nights had it watched for me in that forsaken place? And how did it know that one day I would come there?

Rose screamed.

A moment later she ran forward, and then she was diving through the bushes before I could stop her, and when she came out she was laughing and laughing and she said, 'It's Sarah's star! It's Sarah's star!'

As if I didn't know it was Sarah's star.

★ ★ ★

134

There is very little more to tell about the time we spent on the moor that day. It was night, and we were still alone, but we were on a proper track to the road at last, and Rose was no longer frightened. She was not a bit afraid of Sarah's star. Rose has never been one to abandon her friends. Not like me.

Rose was determined to bring the balloon with us, although I asked her and asked her to leave it.

'It has half gone down,' I said, 'and the writing is all worn off.'

'It is just what I need,' said Rose, and she insisted on bringing it. She found she could use it to catch the reflections of the headlights of cars on the road, and this turned out to be quite useful because one of the headlights she caught was Oscar's. Or rather, Oscar's big brother Alex's. He had come back with Oscar to help start the car, and they had been driving up and down looking for us. 'Alex was just about to call out Mountain Rescue when we saw something shining way out on the hill and guessed it was you,' said Oscar. He did not say, 'Sorry I abandoned you so casually on that lonely road,' or 'I have worried so much,' or even 'Are you cold?' He said, 'Superb stars tonight! What's that you've found, Rose?'

'It's Sarah's star,' said Rose.

I had not told Oscar everything that had happened

the night I took the balloon to Sarah's house, but I had told him a bit. Enough to make him stare first at the balloon and then at me with a very startled face indeed.

'That is seriously weird,' he said, and then he glanced upwards and asked, 'Ever felt watched?'

Watched? This week I have felt more than watched. I have felt haunted.

Rose had overheard Oscar.

'Watched?' she repeated, and she looked up at the sky like Oscar had done. 'Who is watching us?' she asked, shivering and shivering. 'Who?'

'Nobody,' said Oscar, reassuringly. 'Nobody, Rose. There's no one up there but the people in the stars.' And then he took off his top jacket and wrapped it round her shoulders, and all the way back along the track he told Rose stories about the people in the stars. Rose loves it when people tell her stories, and Oscar told her about the seven little sisters who were turned into doves, and the Great Bear and Orion who was there because his girlfriend, having got him into terrible difficulties on Earth, cleverly got him out of them again when she had the bright idea of lifting him safely into heaven and reshaping him out of stars. Rose, for whom no solution can be too spectacular, was very pleased with this idea. 'How good!' she exclaimed, and then she ran ahead with the balloon, trying to fly it like a kite and singing, 'How good, how good!'

'I don't know if it was *that* good,' remarked Oscar. 'I think she did the best she could in the circumstances, but I don't suppose anything was ever quite the same again.'

No, I don't suppose it was.

I had thought I could escape from what had happened the last time I saw Sarah. I had thought I could just let it go, like I did the balloon.

'Did you really?' asked Oscar, when in my unhappiness I explained this to him, and the astonishment and disbelief in his voice made me feel worse than ever.

'Dear, oh dear!' said Oscar, and then (without being told) he changed the subject.

Petrol started the Icon (clever Rose) but Alex waited (in his normal car) to follow us home in case anything else went wrong. He took Rose with him.

'You will like my car much more than my brother's,' he told her. 'It has heat. And if you come with me then Saffy can shout at Oscar as much as she likes.'

Rose went with him without any fuss. I could see

that she was exhausted. Alex strapped her in the back and she went to sleep at once.

So that is how we went home, but I did not shout at Oscar. We did not say one word to each other all the way back until just before we got to Sarah's house. Then Oscar asked, 'What about if I drop you here?' and I said, 'Yes.'

Can't Stop There

'You can't stop there!' said Rose. 'You have not said what happened when you went to Sarah's house.'

When I went to Sarah's house Sarah's mother answered the door, but Sarah was close behind her.

The last time I had seen Sarah's mother, she had shouted, 'Saffron, come here and help me!' and I had run away.

I was prepared for anything except welcome.

Sarah's mother's face lit into a smile and she opened the door wide and stepped back to let me in and exclaimed, 'Saffron! Come in at once! You look frozen! How wonderful to see you, *isn't it*, Sarah?'

'I don't know,' said Sarah, with the most peculiar expression on her face.

'Sarah!'

'Well, it depends,' said Sarah. 'Like, have you come to

operate (Florence Nightingale) or to chuck a few more of my possessions out of the window, or is this just a friendly call? I notice your eyes are straying to the Swiss army knife drawer.'

'Behave yourself, madam!' said her mother, hitting her across her bottom with a rolled up copy of *Vogue*. 'The sooner you are back at school the better, and don't forget the hundred times Saffron has been there for you. I am going to make you both hot chocolate.'

And then she shoved us into the sitting room and left us there together and we looked at each other.

Sarah's mother came in and plonked down a tray of mugs and left again. I don't know why it was suddenly hard to speak, but it was.

'You're better,' I said at last.

'Yes,' agreed Sarah, and then she said, 'Mum's right. There were a hundred times.'

'There should have been a hundred and one,' I said. 'I'm just no good—'

'Yes you are!'

'. . . with imminent death . . .'

'Imminent death!' exclaimed Sarah. 'I wasn't anywhere close . . .' Then she stopped, and I could see her remembering and thinking that even if she hadn't been close, she had been close enough.

'I'm sorry I scared you,' she said. 'I was scared myself.

140

I don't blame you a bit for running off. I'd have run off myself if I could. How was it that it changed so much that afternoon, Saffy, from funny to scary?'

'It was that balloon,' I said, and she agreed at once.

'Yes, it was that balloon.'

'I didn't like it from the start.'

'You saved my life when you got rid of it!'

'I didn't get rid of it though,' I told her. 'You don't know what happened next.'

Then I told Sarah about the Icon, and the moor, and I told her about Rose and her fear of white vans and the way she ran across the hillside in Oscar's hat. I told her about Oscar and the way he looked at me when he heard how I tried to forget about Sarah. I even told her about the Pleiades and the Great Bear and Orion who was made out of stars. And I tried to tell her how cold it had been. At last I told her about how we found her balloon, and how Rose had exclaimed, 'It's Sarah's star!'

'You should drink your choc,' said Sarah, gently.

'Sarah,' I said, 'what do you think? Do you think we are all there is in the world? Human beings – top of the food chain. Or do you think we are absolutely nothing? Random specks on a lump of rock, spinning round a fire. Or do you think we are like the toys of a kid who owns too much? Played with now and then and forgotten in between.'

Still Can't Stop There

'You still can't stop there,' said Rose. 'You have forgotten my sky.'

How could I have forgotten Rose's sky? Rose's black cardboard patchwork sky with the unsatisfactory back.

Rose's Sky

Rose no longer has a problem about the back of the sky. Oscar solved it for her. He said, 'Rose, why are you worrying about the back of the sky. The back is irrelevant. The real sky has no back.'

This pronouncement made Rose very happy.

I was at Sarah's house a long time – so long that when I got home Rose was in bed, and Oscar and Alex (remember Alex?) had gone. The balloon had gone too, or at least it wasn't a balloon any more. It was a thousand silver diamonds spread out on Rose's sky.

'We snipped it up,' said Rose, who had come down in her pyjamas when she heard me in the kitchen. 'It was Oscar's idea. He said to tell you that it was the best thing he could think of doing, under the circumstances. Do you like it?'

'Yes,' I said, because there I was: SAFFRON, spelled out in stars across the sky.

Now Can I Stop?

'Now you can *nearly* stop,' said Rose kindly. 'After Alex.'

(Remember Alex?)

Rose fell so deeply asleep in Alex's car that he had to unstrap her and carry her indoors before she woke up.

And so he met Caddy.

Ever since she first started disappearing from the doorstep, Caddy has believed in love at first sight.

'Is that all you are going to say?' demanded Rose, incredulously.

Yes.

PROBABLY THE
REAL THING

by

Cadmium Casson

Probably The Real Thing

The first time I saw Alex, he was carrying Rose. She was covered in mud and fast asleep, and I could see at once that her usual effortless ability to charm other people's boyfriends was not working here. Alex was holding her as far away from himself as possible, as if she was a dirty pair of boots.

'Where do you want her putting?' he asked, and I hurried to clear a patch of sofa for him. Among the things lying there was a book by Konrad Lorenz on animal behaviour.

Alex dumped Rose and picked it up.

'Who's reading this?' he asked in an astonished but pleased voice (like someone who has found bubble bath and clean towels in a caveman's hut).

'Me,' I said.

'Classic!' said Alex. 'Absolute authority! Classic!'

I was amazed. I thought he must be joking. Outside

of University I had never met anyone who would recognise darling Konrad as an absolute authority. Or a classic. Or even as a human being.

And so I stared at Alex (much taller than Michael, blue eyes, coffee-coloured wavy hair, daft moustache, no jewellery).

And Alex stared at me.

Then Rose woke up and started spreading mud about and Mum rushed in and began flapping her hands and loud music came suddenly from Indigo's room upstairs.

'Come out,' said Alex, grabbing me.

'Where?' I asked.

'Anywhere,' said Alex.

That is how I was swept away by Alex, and it seemed to me from the start that he was probably the Real Thing at last.

My family were very unimpressed by Alex, and they refused to take our relationship seriously. Saffy and Sarah invented a new name for him. They called him the Big Game Hunter, which was utterly unfair. Of course Alex is not a big game hunter; he is a wildlife photographer.

'Same thing,' said Saffron. 'Shoots animals. Don't get so involved, Caddy. He's tough. Ask Oscar if you don't believe me. Or maybe you should just count the notches on his telephoto lens.'

'Don't forget,' put in Sarah, 'that you thought Michael was the Real Thing too.'

'Yes, and look what happened to him!' added Saffron.

'Dumped!' said Sarah. 'Poor Michael. I bet someone else will have snaffled him by now! He was extremely snafflable! I wonder where he is.'

Saffron said that he still sent postcards to Rose, and that she expected I could track him down if I tried.

I reminded them that we were talking about Alex.

'All my friends,' I said (I didn't know Michael was still sending postcards), 'think Alex is gorgeous.'

Sarah patted my hand soothingly.

Saffy ignored me completely. 'There was something about Michael,' she said. 'I used to love how he drove that awful little car around, steering with his knees.'

'He was sweet,' agreed Sarah. 'And cool and funny and never boring . . . Are you absolutely sure Alex is the Real Thing, Caddy? Because I have to admit, he told me more about the creative use of long-range lens distortion than I wanted to know last time I saw him. Impossible to shut up! I just had to wait till it ended. Of course, I do understand it is alpha-male coming out in him and it must be very restful sometimes, to be dragged around by your hair. No decision-making . . .'

Then she and Saffy got the giggles, and so did I, because I could see what they meant. We were still giggling when Rose came in.

'What is funny?' asked Rose.

Rose did not look at all herself. From head to bare feet she was a dusty milky-brown colour. There was a very strong smell of chocolate.

'Alex is funny,' said Saffy. 'What are you covered in?'

'Cocoa and talc,' said Rose, admiring herself in the mirror. 'I thought I'd see what it would be like to be all one colour. Mummy helped, but she says I've got to sit on an old cushion if I sit down. What do you think?'

'Fantastic,' we said. 'Superb! Keep over there and don't touch us.'

Rose did a little twirl and a milk-chocolate cloud swirled from the folds of her skirt.

'I wish I could stay like it forever,' she said. 'Especially my hair. I love my hair. Why were you laughing about Alex? He isn't funny.'

'Of course he isn't,' I said. 'You like him, don't you, Rose?'

'I like Michael much more,' said Rose. 'But I can understand why you like Alex, Caddy.'

Darling little dusty Rose.

'He's like Daddy,' said Rose. 'That's why.'

Bother Rose! Bother her! Bother her! She says what she likes, and she does what she likes, and she always gets away with it. It comes from being the youngest. She is spoilt.

Saffy and Sarah were laughing so much I could hardly hear myself speak. I was very furious.

'Alex is not like Dad in any way!' I said. 'He doesn't look like him—'

'He *walks* like him,' said Rose, mincing about in front of the mirror.

'He doesn't think like him!'

'Think?' asked Rose. 'Think about what? I didn't know they thought about anything.'

'And he doesn't *live* like him! Can you imagine Dad spending days and days waiting on a cold soggy rock in piles of seagull poo and everything sticky and salty just waiting for one tiny puffin chick to come out of its hole?'

'Did Alex do that?' asked Rose. 'The poor little puffin.'

Then I slammed out of the room and packed my bag and went back to London. Rose is an absolute pain sometimes.

I heard later that her hair smelled of chocolate for days.

★　★　★

After that time, I stopped listening to my family. They have always treated everyone I went out with as a Big Joke. (Except Michael.)

Over the next few months I saw more and more of Alex.

I mean I saw Alex more and more often.

But I always saw him away from home.

Then I finished at Uni and started doing voluntary work while I decided what to do next. I worked on wildlife reserves where I counted grasshopper populations with schoolchildren, and cleaned up ponds, and collected Dormouse Evidence. And after that I worked in a lovely conservation zoo, where I gave little talks to the public about how nice snakes actually were, and organised zoo trails, and helped plant a butterfly garden.

I did loads of other things too. I loved it.

Alex was always about, or not far away. He was working on something Top Secret that he called his Permission Submission.

Quite often Alex photographed the animals in my zoo. He took especially dramatic pictures of the bears and the mountain lions – which were in wonderful condition, but as tame as poodles.

Which he explained everyone did and it was

all part of the game and not cheating.

It took him a long time to explain why it was not cheating to me, and I am glad Rose, for instance, never knew anything about it. Because I should never have been able to explain why it was not cheating to her.

Anyway, Dad liked Alex. He even helped him organise an exhibition of his photographs. It turned out to have exactly the same atmosphere as one of Dad's exhibitions. Very successful.

'I think we should be quite proud of ourselves,' said Dad.

He updated the family at home on this latest triumph. He also told them that it was nice to see me happy at last.

They spared me nothing.

'Great news, Caddy!' said Saffron, speaking on the telephone. 'You are happy at last! Rose and I want to know when you were ever not, except when you dumped Michael.'

'Oh shut up,' I said.

'But we feel you ought to know that what Alex produces is not exactly art. Just in case you were looking for an excuse to end the relationship.'

'I'm going to marry him,' I said. 'So ha ha!'

Then there was a silence so long that I thought she must have fainted.

But she hadn't.

She had just stopped laughing.

Alex was quite surprised when I told him that I was going to marry him, because I had not been very enthusiastic when he mentioned it before.

'Why did you change your mind?' he asked suspiciously.

'Because I like you so much,' I said, hugging him.

'Oh good,' said Alex. 'I didn't think you could have heard.'

'Heard what?' I asked, but he just looked smug and asked which I would prefer, a boring conventional ring, or an Adopted Animal for Life – and of course I chose the animal, especially if it could be a gorgeous otter. I had been allowed to look after the otters recently and they would have been my favourites, only I do not have favourites.

However, this hope was dashed.

'Can't stand otters,' said Alex. 'They are too quick. And either you are fighting with reflections or else the little buggers duck. Have a lemur; they're quite photogenic.'

So I agreed.

'Darling Alex,' I said, passionately embracing him.

'Good old Cad,' said Alex, passionately embracing me back. 'They bite like rattlesnakes too.'

'What do?'

'Otters.'

I was quite determined that our married life should not start with otter problems, so I changed the subject and suggested that we go to my zoo at once and tell the news to the animals, and Alex very nicely agreed. He took a camera (of course) and said he would photograph their reactions.

We told the big silverback gorilla first, and he was absolutely delighted and wanted to hug us both. But thankfully there was bulletproof reinforced glass in between. Then we mentioned it to the otters, and I am sorry to say they turned their backs and dived.

'Told you so,' said Alex.

The Indian elephants listened and swung their trunks as if it was all very amusing, but their little reddish eyes looked preoccupied, as if they saw far into the future. Elephants are like that. Their body language tells one story and their eyes another, and I think probably the truth is somewhere in between.

None of the other animals showed any surprise at all.

'They have seen it coming,' I said. 'The meerkats have been gossiping about it for weeks.'

Alex gave me one of his Please Do Not Anthropomorphise The Animals looks. (It is something he feels very strongly about, and he would like to have it written on notices and stuck round all zoos. Alex says it is absolutely ridiculous to anthropomorphise *any* animals and *all* children under the age of fourteen. This is another thing that I am glad Rose knows nothing about.)

However, it was a lovely afternoon, and we hardly argued at all. It was wonderful to be with someone who liked animals as much as I did. None of my other boyfriends ever showed the slightest interest (if we forget chinchilla Patrick). Michael simply did not give a toss.

'They don't bother me,' Michael said once. 'And I don't bother them. I don't shove them in cages or stick them on leads. I don't poke my nose into their private lives or squash them on the roads – except one suicidal squirrel, which I am sorry you had to witness (although I promise he went to heaven). I admit I do eat them, but so do you.'

Michael had only one weak spot where animals were concerned, and that was for big dogs. He liked big dogs. When he met one he would say, 'Hello mate.'

This gave me hope that he might get on equally well with other biggish animals, like bears and lions and camels, but I never got a chance to find out. And now I never will.

Oh well.

It did not take long to arrange for me to become the Adopted Owner of a Lemur for Life, and when I was, Alex said, 'Now it is all official, I will tell you what I would not tell you before. Do you mind if I photograph you as I do, because I think it will be spectacular?'

But I would not agree to this.

'Oh well,' said Alex, 'it will save you having to get changed and the light is not that good anyway.'

Afterwards, he said he was glad he had not bothered, because all I did was stare at him with my mouth hanging open.

'And I thought I'd come up with the most spectacular honeymoon on the planet,' he grumbled.

'Yes!' I said. 'Yes. Alex darling, you have! The most spectacular! On the planet! Ever! Yes, you have!'

And he really had.

Straight away after this I went home, to see how they were bearing the thought of a new member of the family, and to arrange a wedding spectacular enough to match the honeymoon.

I wondered what sort of reception I would get.

Alex's family had been pleased. ('Pleased-ish,' said Alex.) Dad had been delighted. He said, 'This is One Thing we must do Properly,' and offered to arrange the whole wedding. I had been to enough of his exhibitions to know better than to accept that. (Darling Dad has not got much in the way of party spirit.) So I said he needn't worry so long as he didn't mind paying. And he agreed, and put a limit on my budget so high that I had to make him write it down before I believed it. So that was all right.

All this was very positive, but it was not the same when I got home.

Mum cried. She cried because I was grown up and not her little girl any more. She cried because if I married Alex I definitely could not marry Michael, unless I went to live in somewhere like Nepal where to have two husbands was allowed (she said). And she cried most of all because she would have to help arrange the spectacular wedding and she had no idea where to begin.

Luckily, while she was still snuffling away and blowing her nose, Sarah's mother came round. Sarah's mother is the Head of a very posh school and she is kind and funny and very, very efficient. She makes lists. If you asked Sarah's mother to organise the evacuation of the planet she would say, 'I'll just need to start a new list.'

This wonderful woman BEGGED to help with my wedding.

So, bliss.

But I was still not looking forward to seeing Saffy and Indigo and Rose. Saffron's reaction on the phone (unbroken silence) made me fear the worst. And I could not face it. It was Saffy's going on and on at me that made me say I was going to marry Alex in the first place.

No it wasn't.

I would have done anyway.

Of course.

Because he is so wonderful.

And when I said I would marry him, do not forget that I didn't even know that his Top Secret Permission Submission had been successful and that we would therefore be able to have the most spectacular honeymoon on the planet.

I was going to marry him anyway, without that.

Which proves he is the Real Thing.

Which I knew anyway.

I wished Saffy and Indigo and Rose thought he was the Real Thing too, but I knew they didn't. I knew they were going to be awful and talk about Michael all the time, and start Mum off crying again when she had just stopped.

'Leave them to me!' said Sarah's angelic mother, when I told her all this, and she whisked a new blank pink-covered notebook out of thin air, wrote CADDY'S WEDDING on the front, and turned to the first page.

SAFFRON
SARAH
INDIGO
ROSE

she wrote.

'I will catch them after school and invite them to supper,' she said cheerfully. And then she bracketed all their names together and wrote: CONTROL.

And somehow she did. Because when they all burst in that evening (stuffed with Sarah's mother's cooking) they didn't mention Michael once.

They were unnaturally gentle and restrained.

Except right at the end of the evening, as Sarah was going home, Indigo asked, 'What has Alex got, Caddy, that no one else in the world has?'

Then they were all very quiet, waiting for an answer.

'Permission to photograph wild pandas in Western China,' I said.

Rose marched out, slamming the door very hard.
Saffy and Indigo looked at each other and sighed.
'That's it, then?' said Sarah.
'Yes,' I said, bravely. 'That's it.'

DON'T SAY A WORD

by

Rose Casson

Class 4

Chapter One
Hot Gossip
(Part 1)

Sometimes, especially on Fridays when she is in a good mood because two days away from us (Class 4) will be coming soon, Miss Farley does not start lessons straight away. Instead she says, 'Right then, team! Ere we resume our exile in the brain-numbing wastes of Key Stage 2 Literacy Hour, let us have a little Hot Gossip.'

(Do not think Miss Farley always talks like that, because she doesn't. Only on the rare happy days when she has had her eyebrows professionally tidied and is feeling hopeful about the weekend. Otherwise she is an extremely gloomy person. This was hard to get used to when we first knew her. On days when we were feeling particularly thick and sleepy, her sudden despairing yelps of 'How Did It Come To This?' used to make us jump. Now they do not bother us. We have grown quite fond of her. But she has many bad habits. One of the worst of these is the way she has of labelling all conversations not started by herself as Yattering.)

The Friday that I am remembering now, was one of Miss Farley's Good Mood days. Because of this, for a little while the rules were changed and Yattering was officially allowed.

'Five minutes,' said Miss Farley, and she unfastened her watch and laid it down on the desk so that she could time the five minutes to the second. By the time the watch was in position there were twenty-eight arms straining vertically into the air, with muscles so taut their owners' elbow joints were slightly dislocated and their armpits felt unnatural.

'Miss! Miss!' begged the many owners of these arms, their faces taut with pain and gossip. 'Ask me!'

It was always the same on Hot Gossip days. There is never time for Miss Farley to ask everyone who would like to speak, but she always tries to be fair, calling out people's names from all over the room. (Miss Farley has invented a second line of defence that she produces at the end of the session for those people who are still unheard.)

It never matters which name Miss Farley calls out;

she does not even have to look up and see which hands are waving. Any name will do; everyone always has Hot Gossip.

Nearly everyone. That morning it was everyone, except me.

Thus (a word very highly thought of by Saffron and Sarah), that Friday we heard all about:

1. Kiran's uncle's New-but-he-bought-it-secondhand Haunted Car.

2. The school caretaker's unpleasantness about the state of Kai's shoes.

3. The return of Molly's cat after nearly twenty-four hours in the Wild. Molly had given up hope of ever seeing her again. (Molly gives up hope very quickly.)

4. Inside information about the disallowed Arsenal goal on Wednesday night.

5. The loss of Alice's back tooth in the playground before bell, which she had been unable to communicate to anyone, owing to being repeatedly told to get into line and stop talking, even though she was pouring blood. That tooth was a big financial loss to Alice as she planned to use it to extort pound coins from three different sources: separated parents and her gran, who believes that the tooth-fairy lives in a mug on the mantlepiece (which is where she puts her grandchildren's teeth, along with paperclips, small

coins, elastic bands, odd stamps and half-eaten packets of sweets).

Not that Alice's tooth would have stayed there long, because Alice would have fished it out again as soon as her gran's back was turned. It would have been stored in the pink-velvet-lined plastic box with the rest of Alice's collection of fallen-out teeth. Alice is keeping them safe until she becomes famous.

'Then what?' asked Miss Farley, to whom all this was news.

Then they will be auctioned on eBay to Mad Americans.

Said Alice.

I don't know why all this about Alice's tooth irritated Miss Farley so much, but it did. Perhaps because she realised her chance was gone, and she herself would never be famous and in a position to make money selling unwanted body parts on eBay. Anyway, she looked at her watch and remarked that the going rate for teeth in *her* day was twenty pence *only*, from the *tooth-fairy*, *not* your relations, *no* questions asked, and the tooth gone *forever* afterwards.

'Enlightening though this glimpse of Real Life has been,' went on Miss Farley, beginning to deal out scrap paper (second line of defence) whilst ignoring the groans of disappointment all around her, 'we must soon return to the fantasy world of the National Curriculum. I am sorry you did not all manage to tell your stories. Use the scrap paper to write them down. If there is anything that you feel should have been said, write it down, and I will read it at break with my coffee.'

This is what Miss Farley always promises at the end of Hot Gossip, and it is surprising (considering the loudness of the disappointed groans) how little she is given to read with her coffee.

While Miss Farley dealt out the scrap paper she commented upon the Hot Gossip she had heard, saying, 'The caretaker was quite right, Kai, and if you come to school with your shoes in that state again you will have to wear old plimsolls from the Lost Propery Box. Five team points Molly, for getting your cat back! Football is the most deathly boring game on the planet, I'm not surprised they had to wake the ref up at half-time, poor soul. Well done him, I say, staying awake that long. Anyone need any more scrap paper?'

Only Kiran held out her hand. Hot Gossip is like fairy gold, it disappears under your fingers as fast as you try to write it down. Miss Farley knows this very well. The scrap paper is a brilliant tactic. It works like a gag.

But it did not work on Kiran, who was scribbling away like mad beside me.

'Whatever are you finding to put?' demanded Miss Farley, who had already handed over a whole blank-backed Governors' Report big enough to keep most people going for weeks.

'About my dead aunty,' explained Kiran, talking and writing at the same time. 'Who is haunting my uncle's new secondhand car like I told you. She is saying "Slow down! Slow down!" from the back seat and he says he has had enough of it and is going to trade it in for an ex-demonstration Skoda because you can get them for next to nothing if you don't mind the funny looks. It is my dead aunty that was killed by the quarry lorry, but it really wasn't the driver's fault. She ran right in front of him: that was typical of my aunty, she was always doing things like running in front of lorries. It upset the driver really badly, running her over. We know that and we sent him cards after the inquest to show that we understood. Only it was hard to find the right sort of card. My mum got Blank For Your Own Special Message with a picture of a very calm sea.'

'Thank you Kiran, I wish I hadn't asked,' said Miss Farley, when she could get a word in at last. 'And what is the matter with you this morning, Rose?'

'Nothing,' I said.

'She's upset,' explained Kiran helpfully, 'because her sister is marrying a prat in the morning and she's got to be a bridesmaid in a yellow dress.'

'Gold, not yellow,' I said.

'Gold,' agreed Kiran, now sketching the road plan of the scene of her aunty's death (with skid marks). 'Gold. I've seen it.'

'Five team points for being a bridesmaid, then Rose,' said Miss Farley briskly. 'And for goodness' sake, stop moping. Thousands of people make unsuitable marriages every day, and if you feel that strongly you can always voice your objections at the appropriate point in the service. That is why it is there. What on earth is the matter with you, Alice, jiggling about like that? Do you need to go to the bathroom?'

'Can it be five team points for anyone who finds my tooth and gives it back to me?' asked Alice.

'*One* team point,' said Miss Farley begrudgingly. '*One* team point for anyone who finds Alice's tooth. I suppose. Good grief, look at the time, it is break already! Oh well, I suppose we can always call it Creative Writing. Out you all go, and no pulling out teeth to claim the team point. I shall know if you've done it, Kai, and so will Alice!'

Chapter Two
Why I Did Not Feel
Like Hot Gossip

It is time to explain about Michael.

Michael was my sister Caddy's boyfriend. That sounds like Caddy only ever had one boyfriend. Nothing could be further from the truth: she had dozens. But Michael was the only one that mattered.

We were all very, very fond of Michael and we encouraged him in his plot to marry Caddy, but Caddy did not encourage him. When it came to a choice between marrying him and dumping him, she dumped him. Poor Michael. Caddy said she did not think she was the marrying sort. She has changed her mind since, I am sorry to say.

'A pity you could not marry him yourself,' remarked Kiran once, a long time ago, when this first happened.

Yes.

A lot of people think there is only one person in the world for each person to marry, but Kiran and I do not agree. We can both think of quite a lot of people we would not mind marrying. Michael is one of them.

'But you are nine and Michael is twenty-seven. Three times older,' continued Kiran, who does maths naturally in her head. 'So, no good. Although better than when you were six and he was four times older. Or when you were three, and he was seven times—'

I banged Kiran on the head with my reading folder to make her shut up (sometimes you have to do this). And I told her that if I was ninety instead of nine (even though Michael would then be one hundred and eight and therefore, as Kiran remarked, only one point two times older) it would make no difference. Because Michael loved Caddy, not me, and always did, and I think he always will.

Right now, Michael is away with his friend Luke. They are travelling on motorbikes round Europe. This is Luke's way of curing Michael's broken heart. They have been gone for ages, more than a year, so I know it has not worked yet.

I am ten now. That is how long it has been. Michael went away just before my ninth birthday.

★　★　★

I had not seen him for a while, and then one Saturday, about a week before he left, he turned up. He came specially to see me. We went for a walk.

I had my new trainers on for the first time, and their whiteness was amazing. The streets were all end-of-summer-dusty, with piles of dead leaves and paper rubbish drifted into heaps, and I scuffled through them, so as to get a bit of dust on my trainer glow and dim it down a little. I felt happy. I like autumn. I thought of the days that were coming. There would be those early-morning cobwebs that appear everywhere on foggy mornings, and then disappear so quickly you have hardly time to believe in them. Sarah's mother would begin cooking her Sunday Lunches again, and invite us round. There would be the lovely coldness in the air that makes running easier than walking. Daddy would come and measure my height on the kitchen wall and be amazed at how much I'd grown, like he always does on my birthday.

'Do you think I've got much taller this summer?' I asked Michael.

'Much,' said Michael. 'First thing I noticed when I saw you. What do you want for your birthday?'

'Nothing,' I said.

'Now, Rosy Pose, come out of those leaves and don't be useless!' said Michael. 'How can I give you nothing?

Do you seriously expect me to buy nothing, wrap up nothing, stick a gift tag on nothing, send a card saying: I really hope you like your nothing, and lie awake worrying that the nothing I got you was just the right colour nothing that you always really wanted? Have a heart!'

So I thought a bit, and said, 'Chalk,' and explained about the chalk you can buy in tubs on the market, all different colours and very fat sticks.

'Chalk,' said Michael. 'OK, I'll get you chalk.'

So that was settled, and I was pleased because chalk is only a pound a tub and Michael has very little spare money and I didn't want him using it up on me. But he could afford a pound.

Then we talked about a lot of things, like whether one day you would be able to buy distressed trainers like you can jeans. And we went to see Mummy's exhibition of paintings in the library which was mysteriously called 'Pictures from the Edge' and was very careful drawings of letterboxes and parked cars and streetlights and water running down drains, and Michael said he could not see why she had called it that at all, and neither could I at the time. But by the end of that day I could.

Also we bought coffee for Michael, and popcorn for both of us, and an orange shirt for Michael off a market stall (which he said he would hang in the rain until it faded to a reasonable colour), and a hat for me in case it snowed. Then we went into a bicycle shop and chose which bikes we would like best if we were buying bikes, and after that to the music shop where I got a silver hologram guitar pick to send to my friend Tom in New York. And then we went home, not treading on cracks, and I was perfectly happy until Michael said, 'I'm leaving on Monday, Rosy Pose.'

Then I cried.

'Don't be daft, Rose,' said Michael. 'I'll be back. You know I will. I'll be back to marry Caddy, just like we arranged.'

I still cried.

'Look after this for me,' said Michael, pushing the box containing Caddy's diamond and platinum engagement ring into my jacket pocket. 'And don't let Caddy marry anyone else while I'm gone!'

Then he picked me up and he hugged me till it hurt, and before I had time to say one word he was hurrying very quickly away, back along the road we had just come down together. I know now why he was rushing: he wanted to be there before the shops shut. On my birthday I had two presents from Michael. One was a tub of chalk. The other was the bike I had chosen in the bicycle shop.

* * *

Those pictures of normal everyday things that Mummy drew really are pictures from the edge. The edge between happy times and sad. Sometimes you do not know the everyday times are happy until you fall off the edge. And then you want them back, but it is too late. I thought it was just a normal afternoon with Michael until it stopped. And then I saw that it had been a picture from the edge.

On my birthday, Mummy gave me new jeans with hand-embroidered patches. Daddy had bought me a silver bear with an alarm clock in its stomach. Caddy sent me a dream-catcher. Indigo gave me the old denim jacket with the furry collar that he had when he was ten, and a CD he had made of all my favourite songs. Tom sent me a door knocker for my bedroom door. Saffron and Sarah bought me glass paints, so that I can paint on windows.

Michael's bike was dark blue and silver. It came with lights and a bell and a hooter and a lock and a dark blue and silver cycle helmet. No one in my family had ever had a new bike before. I can ride it in the park, and to Sarah's house, and along the cycle track to school.

I did not want Michael to give me anything as big as

a bike, and I ran wailing all through the streets of the town to his house, to tell him so. But he had gone.

That was in the autumn that I was nine, and now more than a year has gone by and it is summer again. Caddy has finished University ages ago. Michael and Luke are still not home.

The last thing Michael said to me was, 'Don't let Caddy marry anyone else while I'm gone!'

Tomorrow Caddy is marrying Alex, and I am to be a bridesmaid in a gold dress.

So no wonder I do not feel like Hot Gossip.

Chapter Three
Listening to Kiran

Kiran is my best friend, and I cannot imagine what school would be like without her. And her stories.

Listening to Kiran is very dangerous. It was Kiran and her stories that caused Mummy to be nearly struck by lightning in the shed. But while Kiran is telling a story you do not remember how dangerous they can be; you just listen.

Back to Hot Gossip Friday.

By the time the Hot Gossip was finished it was break time. Nobody was very eager to go out (except Alice to look for her tooth). The weather was icy cold with grey skies, but they sent us out saying, 'It is June! Go outside and enjoy it!'

So we did. At least, we went outside. The playground looked very dull, with all the boys wrestling over a split football, and the girls in huddled groups round the edge. Miss Farley was on break duty. She was sitting on the Friendship Stop. This is a curved wooden seat where you are supposed to sit if you haven't any friends. There is a notice over the top saying: FRIENDSHIP STOP, so you cannot pretend you just plonked down casually to have a rest. The idea is that if you sit there someone will notice you and come along to rescue you and be your friend (at least until the bell goes). It does not always work. A lot depends on how often you sit there, and who it is that comes to your rescue. In our school it is nearly always the same girl, and if she has rescued you before, she says, 'What is the matter with you? You are always here! That is so weird! What will you give me to tell everyone you're my best friend?'

Most people keep out of the way of the Friendship Stop unless they are desperate, but Miss Farley does not.

That morning she headed straight for it, with her mug of coffee, and her big coat and scarf, and black hat pulled down over her eyes, and Kiran's very long description of the death of her aunt on the back of the Governors' Report. She read between sips of coffee and glaring round the playground over the rim of her mug, watching for trouble. Sometimes while she was reading, she snorted. Kiran watched her suspiciously from a distance.

'She thinks it's funny!' she said crossly. 'She doesn't take any of us seriously. Got any crisps?'

I offered her the half a packet of smoky bacon she had turned down the day before, but she said she was still a vegetarian (she had been all week) and then she wandered off to show some girls how to do handstands against the wall. She is very good at this, and so am I, but I had a skirt on and I couldn't remember which knickers, so I did not join in. Besides, I was thinking about Caddy's wedding in the morning. What did Miss Farley mean when she said I could always voice my objections at the appropriate point in the service?

Miss Farley and I made friends long ago, when she put her pens in a cup of cold coffee and was nice about a disaster that happened in the Reading Corner. So I went and sat down next to her on the Friendship Stop.

'Very kind of you, Rose, but I am bearing up,' said Miss Farley. 'What are those boys stamping on? The little gang in the corner?'

'Only a trick bomb,' I told her. 'They are on offer this week at the joke shop but I think they are damp. Miss Farley—'

'I suppose I ought to stop them,' said Miss Farley, 'but I'll leave it a bit longer. If they succeed in igniting anything major we will be able to get warmed up at least. I hope you plan to wear a good thick woolly vest under your bridesmaid's dress tomorrow, Rose. I think you will need it.'

It is no good arguing with Miss Farley about vests; she is obsessed with them and whenever we get changed for PE she says, 'Where are your vests? Where are your vests? No wonder you will never let me open a window!'

So I said, 'That is a good idea. Miss Farley—'

'And what is the bride wearing?' asked Miss Farley, not seeming to notice that someone had agreed with her about vests for the first time ever in her life. 'For her Big Day? Or is it a secret? They do sometimes like to make a Big Secret out of it, I've noticed.'

I told her that Caddy's dress was very, very pale yellow, and that she was having orange and yellow and scarlet flowers in her hair and to carry, and a veil with tiny beads the same colour, and scarlet and orange shoes to match.

'Goodness,' said Miss Farley jealously.

'And they are going to the church in a carriage with white horses with feathers the colour of Caddy's flowers stuck on their heads,' I said. 'And me and Saffy and Sarah are going in another one, just the same, and everyone else will be in ordinary Rolls Royces and things with scarlet and orange and yellow ribbons. And we have got dried rose petals and rice to throw at them because they don't like confetti at St Matthew's, and afterwards there will be a party with a band and a marquee in Sarah's garden because ours isn't big enough. Sarah's mother has arranged the whole thing. The marquee is there already. It has a real wooden floor. Miss Farley—'

'Sarah's mother must be a saint,' remarked Miss Farley, in a brooding kind of way, not listening to me.

'She likes arranging things, and Mummy hates it, so she let her,' I explained. 'Sarah's mother says it is practice for Sarah's wedding. Miss Farley—'

'Your sister is obviously a very lucky girl,' said Miss Farley. 'I hope she appreciates that fact.'

I said I didn't think she appreciated it at all. Caddy was not a bit like her usual self these days. She was either hunched for hours and hours over maps of China, or prancing around in her wedding shoes trying to cheer herself up.

'Sounds bad,' commented Miss Farley, cheering up a bit herself.

'But whenever I say "Run away Caddy and don't do it!" she shouts at me and bangs the maps about and says it is too late. Miss Farley—'

'It is never too late to come to your senses,' said Miss

Farley, bouncing up and blowing her whistle. 'All you boys stand against the wall! Kiran, fetch the caretaker please! Rose, ring the bell and stop looking so forlorn! Tomorrow will come and it's perfectly obvious to me what will happen, although I know what I would do if I were you. Why on earth is James rolling about like that?'

'He is hurt,' I said, running after her as she hurried across the playground. 'Miss Farley, what would you do if you were me?'

But Miss Farley was not listening any more. She had to bandage up James's twisted ankle because she is a first aider, and then she had to ring his mum to fetch him home because he said he was dizzy, and then she had to write an Accident Report explaining how he had injured his ankle and banged his head while stamping on a trick bomb. She did this during Numeracy Hour, which came after break, grumbling and groaning and asking, 'How Did It Come To This?'

As usual.

She gave us all Revision Worksheets to get on with in silence (she said – although in actual fact we did a lot of groaning too).

'Kiran,' I whispered, while all this moaning was going on, 'did you hear what Miss Farley said just before break about Caddy's wedding?'

'When she said you could always voice your objections at the appropriate place in the service?'

'Do you know what she meant?'

'It's what everyone does,' said Kiran, kindly converting all my fractions into decimals for me in my own faked handwriting, which is a very useful thing she had learned to do. 'If they don't think the people getting married should be allowed to do it. That's when they complain. You know, at the bit in the service when the vicar or whoever is doing the umpiring says, "Anyone got any problems before I go ahead?"'

'Do they really say that?'

'Of course,' said Kiran, airily sharing out my pie diagram into slices. 'Yes. Always. They have to. It's the Law. (There! You can colour that in.) How come you never go to weddings, Rose?'

'I do other stuff,' I said, not wanting to say I've never been asked. 'I'm always very busy on Saturdays. I can't fit everything in as it is. Tell me more about the any problems bit.'

'In a minute,' said Kiran. 'Seventeen nines?'

What a ridiculous question.

'Hundred and fifty-three,' said Kiran, without even pausing for breath. 'Because seventeen tens are a hundred and seventy. Nineteen sevens? Hundred and thirty-three. I've been to millions of weddings. The any-problems-before-I-go-ahead bit is the best part of all. At my mum's best friend's sister's wedding, half the church jumped up and started waving their hands in the air. And the first time I was a bridesmaid, the groom fainted at that absolute moment and he had to go and sit on the doorstep with a glass of water and a digestive biscuit, and the vicar said it happened all the time. And at my cousin-with-the-twins's wedding where the twins were the bridesmaids, someone rushed into the church and shouted out, "Could the owner of the white Fiesta with the dog in the back come straight away – you left the handbrake off and it is rolling down the main street and the dog can't drive!" That was my best wedding ever: we all ran outside and took photos of the dog . . .'

I was filled with sudden wild and gorgeous hope. I had always assumed that once Caddy and Alex made it into the church it would be all over. Nobody had told me about this wonderful Last Chance.

Kiran was showing her working in my handwriting. Her dark lashes were lowered, her black hair was parted in one long clean line from front to back, and she was using a ruler. She looked like an angel doing sums. Anyone would have trusted her.

'Haven't you been to any normal weddings?' I asked.

'No,' said Kiran, angelically filling in the missing

numbers in a pattern of squares. 'Even if the bit in church goes OK, the cake falls over or they lose their passports at the airport and have to have their honeymoon at their mum's. At one I went to, all the tiles blew off the church roof when they were taking the photos and only the bride's family were hit. They got taken away in three ambulances and they said it was a Plot. But they usually go wrong ages before the photograph stage. If they get to the wedding at all. There, I've done your whole worksheet. Do you want to play Hangman?'

I did not want to play Hangman, but anyway I did not have the chance because just then Miss Farley pounced on us both. She was very annoyed that Kiran had done my worksheet for me again.

'Some people would call what you two have been doing cheating,' she said. 'What will you do when you are grown up, Rose, and don't have Kiran around to do your work for you?'

I did not reply, because I live with Saffron and Sarah and know a rhetorical question when I hear one, but Kiran said, 'It is all right, Miss Farley. Rose is going to employ me as her PA when she is grown up and then it will not be cheating, it will be delegation. We are practising Life Skills.'

This explanation caused Miss Farley to come very

close to having a tantrum, and she said, 'You get all these answers off TV which you obviously watch far too much.'

Kiran and I did not argue, although we might have, as our TV is always coming loose at the aerial and Kiran's family do not have one at all. (Kiran says they talk to each other instead.)

But it would have been no use telling Miss Farley this, because she was not in the mood. So we put on our Told Off faces (which I do by opening my eyes a bit wider than usual and slightly sucking in the corners of my mouth and Kiran does by pushing her hair behind her ears and blinking too much) and we prepared to wait for Miss Farley to get over it.

At this point a distraction was caused by Kai taking off his shoe and passing it to his neighbour to smell.

So Miss Farley gave up on Kiran and me, but she did not forget entirely. At the end of the lesson she gave me a new blank worksheet to fill in over the weekend by myself. She said, 'I appreciate you will be occupied tomorrow, Rose, but I don't suppose you will have anything better to do on Sunday.'

How right she was.

Chapter Four
Caddy's Wedding

When I arrived home from school that Friday afternoon, Daddy was there.

I was very surprised. I said, 'What are you here for?'

And he said, 'For Goodness' Sake, Rose! Who else did you think was going to give Caddy away?'

'Oh, I hate that expression!' said Mummy. 'It is just as if poor Caddy was being got rid of Free To Good Home like we used to have to do with her guinea pigs when we ran out of cages. Hello, Rose darling, I am just rushing out to buy a hat – would you come with me? What's the matter, Bill?'

Daddy was staring at her with his mouth hanging open. He said, 'Are you telling me, Eve, that you haven't got a hat?'

'Of course I'm not,' said Mummy meekly. 'I know I have my woollies and my big blue painty one, but I thought for tomorrow something new would be nice and the market won't be packing up for another hour. Please come, Rosy Pose, because you have Style.'

Daddy took a big deep breath and let it out very slowly.

'Let's rush, Rose,' said Mummy.

So we did.

The hat stall was nearly packed up when we got there and the people running it seemed rather grumpy. They told us that it had been a bad day for hats. 'Too breezy,' said the Hat Man, 'not like proper June and an icy cold wind straight from the melting polar ice cap. Global warming. Might as well call it a day.'

But when the Hat Man and the Hat Man's wife understood that Mummy wanted a new hat for her daughter's wedding in the morning, they changed completely. They unpacked their whole van and a mirror and flask of tea and some ginger nuts, and it turned into a sort of visit.

'It'll be your turn before you know where you are, Madame Fernackerpan,' said the Hat Man's wife to me. 'Got your eye on anyone yet?'

I said I had got my eye on two or three – but not to marry, to go off with when I wanted someone to go off with.

'What a cracking idea,' said the Hat Man, and Mummy and the Hat Man's wife agreed.

Then Mummy found a hat that smelled wonderful, just like dry grass, and looked like it was beautifully woven out of hay, and started crying.

'This is the hat I shall have to watch poor little Caddy get married in,' she cried. 'Rose, have you got a tissue, darling? Where did I put my purse down?'

The Hat Man and his wife were very kind. They took the £3.49 label off the hat and put it in a pink-and-white striped carrier bag and said it was free. And they hugged Mummy and said to come and let them know how it went, and they had thought of going in for kids themselves at one time but settled for King Charles Spaniels in the end and on the whole they were glad.

So that was Mummy's hat.

When we got home, Daddy was pacing up and down the pavement in front of the house saying, 'What else has not been done?'

Sarah's mother was with him, trying to calm him down, and saying, 'Everything is going to be perfect!'

And Mummy went snuffle snuffle snuffle, and got out her pink-and-white bag, and Sarah's mother said it was a dream of a hat. Superb.

'Mine is simply over the top,' she said, sniffing Mummy's in an admiring kind of way. 'But when will I get the chance again? Sarah will never take anyone seriously enough to marry them. In fact, she never takes anything seriously! Look at that rabbit! I ask you! When Caddy will be on her way to China in two days' time (but I will see you do not get Landed). I must dash!'

And she did, while Daddy was still asking, 'What rabbit? What rabbit?'

Poor Daddy. But it would have been useless trying to explain about the rabbit, so we just said, 'Oh never mind,' which made him mad.

That night was chaos in our house.

Caddy's wedding dress and the bridesmaids' dresses filled the whole of upstairs. Daddy's clothes for the weekend filled the living room. At any point in time someone was always crying or feeling ill, except Indigo. Indigo was the only calm person in the house. He calmly told Daddy that he would not be seen dead in a suit, calmly displayed the clothes he intended to wear in the morning (jeans and a black T-shirt and a very nice jacket from Oxfam), and then calmly went out. He was going to see his friend David the drummer who, Indigo said, could be absolutely relied on not to talk about weddings, or pandas, or the inoculations you need to go to China, or in fact anything except drums.

Nobody took much notice of me, but I did not mind. There was plenty of food in the fridge so I made myself a ham and baked bean sandwich and escaped upstairs. As I went I heard Caddy wail, 'I can't believe this wedding is going to happen in the morning.'

I thought of the state of our house that night, and Mummy's tears at the hat stall, and Kiran's stories of wedding disasters. And I thought of how Caddy had loved Michael so much that she had never put him in her address book because she knew she would never forget him, and I couldn't believe this wedding was going to happen in the morning either.

And I was glad.

So.

Skip the night, when nobody slept.

Skip the morning when two hairdressers moved into the house and started acting like they owned our heads and we were just allowed to live underneath them, as long as we kept our hands down and did not touch once.

★　★　★

Skip the rabbit, a last-minute wedding present from Sarah to Caddy, which she delivered in a silver box with air holes.

The rabbit had black eye-patches and Sarah had made it a little black jacket and black trousers (which it bit off in seconds).

'It is a practice panda,' said Sarah. 'I thought you could practise creeping up on it and taking photos. I'm awfully sorry, Eve, I didn't have time to house-train it. What'll you call it, Caddy?'

'Alex,' I suggested. 'It looks a lot like him.'

'Rose!' snapped everyone.

'I can't possibly call him that,' said Caddy very nicely (but insanely). 'I have always thought Alex looks ninety-nine per cent Greek god but (face it, darlings) Rose is right. The rest is rabbit, and that's probably why animals love him and let him take their photographs. Pandas, pandas, pandas – I must keep concentrating on the pandas! It is such a good thing Oscar got you and Rose lost on that horrible moor, Saffy, otherwise I might never have met Alex and I'd have missed the pandas.'

'You wouldn't have met him anyway,' said Sarah, 'if Indigo hadn't done that disco to impress me (I was frightfully impressed, Indy) and got Saffron and Oscar together! Pity it didn't last a bit longer, Saff.'

'We are giving each other Space,' said Saffron.

'You are so right!' said Caddy. 'No, you're not! Pandas, pandas, pandas! Aren't my shoes perfect!'

'Yes,' said everyone. 'They are absolutely gorgeous, Caddy.'

Skip the ride to St Matthew's in the carriage, which was brilliant and over much too soon.

Skip the crowd at the church gates, waiting to see what we looked like. Kiran was one of the crowd. She pushed forward to grab me and say, 'Has anything gone wrong yet?'

'No,' I admitted. 'I don't know why.'

'It will!' said Kiran cheerfully. 'You wait and see!'

Skip me holding Caddy's train, and Sarah walking all the way up the aisle between Saffy and Indigo, and the lovely way everyone clapped when she made it.

Skip Alex smirking at my trainers (which were white and matched my dress perfectly and even Sarah's mother had liked).

Skip 'All Things Bright and Beautiful', Caddy's favourite hymn, and a lot of talk by the umpire, I mean vicar, telling us who was here (Caddy and Alex) and why they were here (to get married) and why we were here (to watch) and what marriage was for (Babies, he said – wrong, should have been pandas).

All this went on for ages.

I looked around. I was beginning to get very worried. This was not like any of the weddings Kiran had described. Nobody had fainted, or run in shouting from the street. Nothing had fallen from the roof. It was all very calm and flower-scented and organised. There was a tremendous feeling of special clothes, and high windows, and stone and oldness. A lot of people smiled at me looking at them, but Daddy (who had Mummy in a very firm grip) mouthed: 'Turn round!'

I was the only one up there with Caddy and Alex. Saffy and Indigo had taken Sarah across to the pews at the front so that she could sit down.

I felt very alone, and I was starting to be frightened. Also I was beginning to think that Kiran was wrong when she said the umpire would get to the anyone-got-any-problems bit, and that would be when everything would happen. Perhaps there would not be an anyone-got-any-problems bit at all. Perhaps the law saying there must be had changed since Kiran last went to a wedding. Perhaps they stopped it, because it caused so much trouble.

I seemed to have been standing there for ages, and I thought that Caddy must be just about married, and that nobody was going to do anything to help me.

And then it came.

The vicar, the umpire, said, 'I am required to ask anyone present who knows a reason why these persons may not lawfully marry, to declare it now.'

THAT WAS IT AT LAST!

I grabbed Caddy's train, in case she was going to want to get away quickly, and I spun round.

Now things were happening. People were shuffling and murmuring. Daddy took a step towards us and then changed his mind and went back. I stared at the audience, who looked very uncomfortable, and I prayed for a rescue and in my mind I shouted, 'Come on! Somebody! Somebody speak!'

Somebody did speak. The sound seemed to come from very high up above my head.

'Please!' they begged, 'Please! Before it is too late!'

And it was me.

'Rose!' gasped Caddy. 'Rosy Pose?'

'I promised Michael—' I began, but I did not get time to finish because Daddy grabbed me. He grabbed me and he stuffed me under his arm and he ran with me all the way down the aisle and through the wooded arches and past the font and out to the porch and he threw me on to the grass in the graveyard and dropped down beside me and gagged me with his hand so I could hardly breathe (not that I cared if I died, right then) and the next thing I knew was Kiran bending over me and Miss Farley racing through the graves looking absolutely terrible and roaring, 'It is all my fault!'

Chapter Five
Maths Worksheet

On Sunday it was quite important for me to get my maths worksheet done. I could not do it on Saturday because I was rather busy in the morning, and most of the afternoon and evening I was at Kiran's house.

It was a very hard worksheet. I had to concentrate. I concentrated on it for most of Sunday, in my bedroom with my door shut so that nobody would distract me. I wanted it to be perfect, and in the end it was.

Or as perfect as I could get it, anyway.

I used an italic nib to write the answers, which made them look very nice, and the pie diagram was beautiful. I shaded in each slice like the petals of a flower. Around the edge of the sheet I drew a border of hexagons in a honeycomb pattern. I put a few bees among the hexagons – not very many, just a few for anyone to find and look at who likes bees.

I think Miss Farley likes bees. Whenever one gets stuck in the classroom she lets it out very carefully.

I hoped Miss Farley would be very pleased with my maths worksheet. I hoped it might put her into a good mood.

Miss Farley had not been in a good mood the last time I saw her. This was my fault. I had an idea that I thought might be a good idea, but in real life it wasn't. In real life it was (as Kiran explained) insane. I should not have tried to push Miss Farley into the church to marry Alex instead of Caddy. Poor Miss Farley. She was not dressed in the right clothes to get married, and none of her friends were there (except Kiran and me), and she was very out of breath because suddenly on that Saturday morning she had had a very strong feeling that something frightful would happen at Caddy's wedding. She had run all the way across the market place to try and prevent it because it is impossible trying to park near St Matthew's on a Saturday.

Anyway, Miss Farley did not want to marry Alex. It was a completely bad idea and it made her very angry and I wish I had not thought of it. I just could not bear the thought of the whole wedding being wasted.

Daddy says nothing was wasted.

★ ★ ★

Daddy can be very awful, but he can be very nice too. The first thing he said after he ungagged me with his hand was, 'Did I hurt you, Rose?'

I was sort of gasping and crying and I could not speak, but I shook my head.

'I think I've ricked my back,' said Daddy, getting up very stiffly. 'But thank heaven nobody has followed us. I've got to go back, Rose, and hold it together. I hope to goodness they carried on . . .'

And then we both looked towards the dark doorway of the porch that led into the church. As we looked, Alex and Caddy and the umpire appeared.

From the church itself came a great whispering hum. It was as if the stone of the walls was murmuring. The murmur grew louder and louder. It was the sound of the people inside wondering what would happen next.

Mummy's face popped up between Alex and Caddy, and then I saw Indigo, and Alex's best man, who was someone I did not know. Alex and the umpire and the best man were talking very fiercely and making quick flat gestures in the air with their hands, like boys in the playground when they are busy fixing a deal. Caddy was nodding; she seemed to be on the side of the umpire and the best man, who were not on Alex's side. Mummy was sniffing her hat.

I saw all this in a second.

The moment all those people appeared, Daddy became heroic. He brushed the grass off his jacket and straightened his shoulders. 'Look after Rose!' he said to Kiran and Miss Farley, and he began to limp towards the church. By the time he got there he had even managed to smile, and he held his arms wide as if he was embracing a huge, special, perfect joke. Then he kissed Mummy and put one arm round Alex and the other around Caddy, and said in his most everything-is-absolutely-wonderful voice, 'Now let's get these two people married!'

'Rose, I think it's going to be all right,' whispered Kiran. 'They're going back in!'

And it was then that I had my good idea, and I jumped up and grabbed Miss Farley and tried to push her after them into the church, but luckily Kiran is stronger than me. Kiran got a good grip on a gravestone with one hand and my flame-coloured sash with the other, and she hung on, hissing, 'Rose, you have gone mad! Rose, you are in shock! Rose, let go of Miss Farley!' And so Miss Farley was able to break free and escape among the tombs. Then Kiran hauled me back to the crowd at the gate, and she said, 'I think we should go back to my house.'

So we did.

* * *

There are no words to say how unreal it felt, walking through the Saturday market in my bridesmaid's dress and trainers to Kiran's house. I remember saying to Kiran, 'I should not be here.'

'No,' said Kiran. 'You shouldn't.'

Kiran's house was full of people talking: her mother and her big brother and her aunt and her grandmother and other people who might have been relations or neighbours, I did not know which. They were all talking. It was amazing. Words surged from every room. They lapped against the walls and furniture. They splashed and showered around us when we opened the door.

Then they saw us and they stopped.

'This is Rose. Do not fuss her!' commanded Kiran, and she steered me up to her room, pushed me in, and asked, 'Rose?'

'Yes?'

'What did you actually *do*?'

It was nice at Kiran's house. They fed me pizza and they lent me clothes and they rang my home and left a message on the answerphone to say where I was, and they told me dozens of stories, and when it was night they made up a blow-up bed for me in Kiran's room and I fell asleep at once. I was very tired.

And in the morning Kiran's father drove me home.

The only person home was Daddy. He still had his ricked back. He walked very stiffly out to Kiran's father and they shook hands through the car window.

'Daughters,' said Kiran's father, raising his eyebrows.

'Yes,' said Daddy, shaking his head.

'Ah!' said Kiran's father, as if he understood everything, and then he drove away.

So there I was, standing in the street with my bridesmaid's dress in a carrier bag.

'Had any breakfast?' asked Daddy.

'Yes thank you,' I said. 'And now I had better get on with my maths worksheet.'

Chapter Six
Hot Gossip
(Part 2)

On Monday morning when I gave Miss Farley my maths worksheet, she laughed until she choked and had to sit down. And then she wiped her eyes and drank the water Kiran brought her and said, 'Right, and now it is time for a little Hot Gossip. Hands down everyone except Rose.'

So I had to tell everyone the amazing true story of Caddy's wedding and I began with Kiran's wedding stories.

'Skip all that,' interrupted Miss Farley. 'We all know Kiran.'

So I went on to Mummy's hat and Sarah's rabbit.

'We haven't got all day,' said Miss Farley. 'Skip the hat and the rabbit.'

She made me skip the carriage ride too, and she would not let me tell the very naughty thing Saffron and Sarah did when they came out of church.

'Cut to the kill,' said Miss Farley. 'You interrupted the proceedings at a critical moment and . . . ?'

'Daddy threw me out and ricked his back,' I said.

'But meanwhile . . . ?'

Meanwhile, in the church, Caddy pulled herself together very quickly. There was dead silence (they told me) after her gasp of 'Rosy Pose?' and the sound of Daddy's footsteps, and the slamming of the door into the porch. And then Caddy said in a very cheerful voice, 'Oh well. Never mind darling Michael, Alex. Let's get it over with.'

But Alex would not get it over with. He demanded to know who the blazes was Darling Michael.

'Just someone I knew,' said Caddy. 'Stop worrying, Alex. This time tomorrow we'll be flying to China. Just think: Pandas, pandas, pandas.'

Alex would not think: Pandas, pandas, pandas. He was very stubborn. He said, 'I am going to have a word with your dad,' and marched off down the aisle leaving Caddy standing at the altar. The best man ran after Alex, and Caddy and the vicar and Mummy and Indigo hurried after the best man. They all caught up with each other in the porch and there they explained to Alex that Michael had disappeared from Caddy's life long, long ago.

'Well, Caddy and the vicar did,' said Indigo, relating this to me on Sunday evening (which was when I finally rejoined my family). 'I kept out of it, and so did Mum.'

'I couldn't help feeling it was never meant to be,' said Mummy, 'Alex and Caddy, I mean. I didn't know what to do, until Bill came back. You were absolutely wonderful, Bill!'

'Can't say I felt it,' said Daddy, who was looking up chiropractors in the Yellow Pages.

'And Caddy was so brave . . .'

'Rose was the bravest,' said Saffron.

Then all my family, from whom I had hidden the whole of that day, looked very kindly at me.

I had thought they would be furious. I had thought they might not speak to me for weeks. I had planned to stay up in my bedroom for ever and only come down for food at night. I would have been up there right then, if I hadn't just discovered I'd been burgled.

'Burgled?' asked Kiran. 'You didn't tell me you'd been burgled!'

'Rose!' snapped Miss Farley. 'Skip the burglary, for

heaven's sake. *Did your sister agree to marry that unfortunate young man or not?*'

'She agreed to marry him,' I said, 'but he didn't agree to marry her back.'

'They have to both agree to get married,' explained Kiran.

'I am aware of that, thank you, Kiran,' said Miss Farley. 'So? Rose?'

'Yes?'

'It's like dragging blood out of a stone!' said Miss Farley. 'WHAT HAPPENED NEXT?'

'Oh,' I said, 'Alex went off to China all by himself in a huff. They had to carry on the wedding without him – which ruined parts of it, Saffy said. But Caddy was all right; Mummy said she'd completely cheered up by the time she got home. And Daddy said as long as Caddy was happy it was all for the best. So.'

'So,' said Kiran cheerfully. 'Sorted!'

'*Sorted!*' repeated Miss Farley.

'By Rose,' said Kiran.

Appendices

Appendix I
The Very Naughty Thing Saffron and Sarah Did When They Came Out of Church

They hijacked one of the carriages with its driver, and they went for a trip all round town in it.

'It was Sarah's idea,' said Saffron. 'But I knew the moment she suggested it that it was absolutely the right thing to do.'

Appendix II
What Happened to all the Food and the Marquee and the Band and all the Stuff at Sarah's House

The food and the band and the marquee were not wasted. Nearly everyone who was at the wedding went on to Sarah's house. Sarah's mother invited them.

'It was quite good fun, in a strange kind of way,' said Indigo. 'Everybody was very cheerful and a lot of people were saying Better Finding Out Late than Never. And Dad had a good time not moaning about how much it had all cost him and making people laugh at Mum's free hat. The only thing was, they didn't know what to do with the cake. Until Sarah's dad said, "It's a cake! Eat it!" So we did.'

Appendix III
What Happened To Caddy

CADDY BURGLED ALL MY POSTCARDS FROM MICHAEL AND DISAPPEARED.

Read on for a sneak preview of Forever Rose,
the Casson Family Finale

After Molly left us Kiran and I walked on together to my house.

At first it seemed that there was no one home. All the windows were dark (I love it when I come home and all the windows are bright) but then we bumped into Mummy outside the back door. She was wearing a sleeping bag like a toga and clutching a hot-water bottle and obviously heading for the garden shed where she paints her pictures, makes private shed-based plans for world peace, and escapes from us, her wonderful family (this time represented by Me).

Kiran and Mummy have met before, so I did not have to explain them to each other.

'Hello, Mrs Casson!' said Kiran.

'Kiran . . . (sneeze) how lovely . . . (sneeze) Call me . . . (sneeze) Eve, darling,' said my mother, her face muffled in a handful of kitchen roll and backing away like mad. 'Rose, I won't kiss you because I think I may have caught something (sneeze-gasp-sneeze). I am going to go and have it in private in the shed . . . (sneeze).'

'Oh!'

'One huge germ,' continued Mummy, pointing to her head to make things quite clear. 'So off I go! Hope you had a lovely day at . . .' (she sneezed so hugely that the sleeping bag fell around her knees) '. . . school?'

'No,' I said. 'It was terrible. I've told you before. It gets awfuller every day.'

But I don't think Mummy heard. She was concentrating on recapturing the sleeping bag. Saffy heard instead. She came out of the house just in time. Saffy is my other sister (ie the one who is not Caddy).

Saffron: seventeen, stunningly beautiful, super-intelligent, and not to be argued with.

'What gets awfuller every day?' she demanded, herding Kiran and me into the kitchen and then rushing about collecting things for Extra Spanish which she does after school two days each week because she is so brainy. 'You're not ill too, are you, Rose? Perhaps you should go and live with Mummy in the shed. Indigo and I could leave you supplies at the door as if you had the plague. Don't look like that, Kiran! She would love it!'

Yes I would.

No school.

It was a wonderful idea and I was about to start fake sneezing straight away when Kiran said, 'She isn't ill at all. It is Mr Spencer that gets more awful every day.'

'Never heard of him,' said Saffron, with her head in her bag.

'Our new class teacher. He doesn't like any of us. Do you know what he said to me last week? He said, "Kiran, you will undoubtedly find yourself in well justified but colossal trouble one day if you do not learn to understand the vital difference between plain fact and paparazzi-style fantasy!" That's what Mr Spencer said. I wrote it down.'

'Tell him less is more when it comes to adjectives,' said Saffron, sounding very uninterested. 'And pass me that blue file, please!'

'He says we are all immature,' continued Kiran (passing it). 'And he says however will Rose manage at Big School in less than one year's time if she cannot read!'

By this time Sarah, Saffron's best friend, had arrived because she does Extra Spanish too. Sarah has a wheelchair that she uses for transport, emotional blackmail in queues, as an occasional weapon, and as a convenient place to hug people from. I got a quick, protective wheelchair hug as she exclaimed, 'Of course Rose can read! What's the man talking about?'

'Books,' explained Kiran.

'Books?'

'You know how Rose doesn't read books? Mr Spencer can't take it. She stares out of the window and it makes him so mad he—'

'*I* didn't know Rose didn't read books,' interrupted Sarah. 'What, never, Rose? Not even at school?'

'Lazy little disgrace!' remarked Saffron.

'You don't know how it is at our school!' I said, defending myself. 'If you finish one book, they make you pick another. And as soon as you finish that, they send you off to the book boxes again. And each book is a little bit harder than the one before. It's called Reading Schemes and it's just like a story Indigo once told me about a dragon with two heads. And when the dragon's two heads were cut off, it grew four. And when they were cut off it grew eight . . .'

'I've never *heard* such rubbish!' said Saffron.

'It's true! Do you know what happened when Kiran finished all the books in the school library last year? They got extra money from the PTA and ordered two hundred more!'

'Actually I was pleased . . .' murmured Kiran.

'So at school now I just—'

'Hand over your school bag!' ordered Saffron.

'. . . usually . . .'

Saffron turned my bag upside down and grabbed a book from the heap of junk that fell out.

'. . . draw.'

But Saffy wasn't listening. She was asking, 'What's this supposed to be? Look, Sarah! What does that awful writing say?'

'History,' said Kiran helpfully, craning to look as Saffron flipped through the pages.

'It's all pictures!' said Sarah, staring at it. 'Give me another! What's this?'

'Science.'

'*It's* all pictures as well! Where's your Maths?'

'Maths?'

'Maths! Numbers! Sums!'

'Probably at school,' I said.

'Ha!' said Saffron. 'I bet it's all pictures too!'

(A bad guess, although I did not say so. My Maths book is all Spaces for Missing Work.)

'Her not reading's the worst,' said Sarah, looking at me in a truly shocked kind of way.

'Well, I'm with Mr Spencer,' said Saffron, bundling all my stuff back together into my bag and handing it to me. '*I* don't know what you're going to do when you start Big School either! Just don't let on you're related to me. We're late, come on, Sarah!'

Slam.

Saffron was gone.

'Rose,' said Sarah, 'not reading's *awful.*'

It's not.

'You've got to change.'

I don't see why.

'I'll help.'

You needn't.

'Don't argue, I'm *going* to,' said Sarah.

Slam.

Oh.

Kiran left almost straight after Saffy. She was late too. There are always loads of people at Kiran's house, waiting for her to come home and wondering where she is. I can remember when it was like that here. The kitchen used to be full. There was never enough space.

There is plenty of space now; a whole houseful.

Where have we all gone?

Mummy is in the shed.

Daddy is in London, being an artist. He says he is getting old.

Caddy, my grown-up sister, has been very elusive for the last year or so. Last heard of she was in Greece, working in a Sea World centre, getting up campaigns to rescue unhappy parrots from unsuitable owners, and trying to get over Michael who was the boyfriend she only fell completely in love with after she had agreed to marry someone else.

Michael is avoiding us. I saw him only the other day, teaching someone to drive. He looked away. Which is not fair, because if anyone was on Michael's side, it was me. Think what I did at Caddy's wedding. (No, don't.)

Saffron. Saffron is on her way to Spanish class.

Indigo, my brother, will be at the music shop in town. He has free guitar lessons from the owner in return for vacuuming the carpets and washing up the day's supply of dirty mugs in the little kitchen at the back.

And

The guinea pigs have been given away.

The hamsters all escaped.

So that is why

This house

Feels so

Empty.